The tank rumbled on, seemingly unstoppable

Bolan pulled the pins on a pair of grenades and charged the armored vehicle.

As he ran into range, his progress was noted and the tank's turret spun to put its gun on him. Bolan threw a grenade. The white phosphorus charge hit the tank square on its slanted front. The vehicle's prow was immediately enveloped in white smoke and streamers of metal skyrocketed. Bolan took a hard left and threw himself down as the tank fired blindly at him. The sonic crack of a shell passed two feet over him, and coax fire followed, but it was scything in the wrong direction. Bolan rose.

Again he sprinted toward the tank. Waves of heat rolled off it from the burning phosphorus on the front deck, but the warrior paid no attention. He jumped and hooked an arm over the 100 mm barrel, letting it carry him toward the bow. The turret continued to turn, and he dropped onto the tank's blackened back deck. A scorched dent the size of a trash can lid cratered the steel, and a smoking hole the size of a fist marked where the grenade had penetrated. Bolan could hear men shouting below, and chemical fire extinguisher squirted out of the opening.

The Executioner unclenched his fist and dropped his second grenade down the hole.

MACK BOLAN ®
The Executioner

The Executioner®
Don Pendleton's
LINE OF HONOR

A GOLD EAGLE BOOK FROM
WORLDWIDE®

TORONTO • NEW YORK • LONDON
AMSTERDAM • PARIS • SYDNEY • HAMBURG
STOCKHOLM • ATHENS • TOKYO • MILAN
MADRID • WARSAW • BUDAPEST • AUCKLAND

Recycling programs
for this product may
not exist in your area.

First edition June 2012

ISBN-13: 978-0-373-64403-2

Special thanks and acknowledgment to
Charles Rogers for his contribution to this work.

LINE OF HONOR

Printed in U.S.A.

If honor calls, where'er she points the way, The sons of honor follow and obey.

—Charles Churchill
1731–1764
The Farewell

Where there are people in need of my help, I will go. Because it is only in keeping up the fight against those who do evil against the innocent—no matter where on this planet they may be—that this war can be won.

—Mack Bolan

THE
MACK BOLAN
LEGEND

Nothing less than a war could have fashioned the destiny of the man called Mack Bolan. Bolan earned the Executioner title in the jungle hell of Vietnam.

But this soldier also wore another name—Sergeant Mercy. He was so tagged because of the compassion he showed to wounded comrades-in-arms and Vietnamese civilians.

Mack Bolan's second tour of duty ended prematurely when he was given emergency leave to return home and bury his family, victims of the Mob. Then he declared a one-man war against the Mafia.

He confronted the Families head-on from coast to coast, and soon a hope of victory began to appear. But Bolan had broken society's every rule. That same society started gunning for this elusive warrior—to no avail.

So Bolan was offered amnesty to work within the system against terrorism. This time, as an employee of Uncle Sam, Bolan became Colonel John Phoenix. With a command center at Stony Man Farm in Virginia, he and his new allies—Able Team and Phoenix Force—waged relentless war on a new adversary: the KGB.

But when his one true love, April Rose, died at the hands of the Soviet terror machine, Bolan severed all ties with Establishment authority.

Now, after a lengthy lone-wolf struggle and much soul-searching, the Executioner has agreed to enter an "arm's-length" alliance with his government once more, reserving the right to pursue personal missions in his Everlasting War.

1

The Sudan

The wind roared through the open door of the helicopter cabin. Mack Bolan's knuckles went white on the grips of the M-134 minigun as he watched the armor-piercing incendiary cannon shells streak past the cabin like green laser lines in the predawn. He shouted into his throat mike to reach Jack Grimaldi in the cockpit. "Jack! Do something!" The Sukhoi Su-25 Frogfoot close air support jet was flying right up *Dragonslayer*'s rear and seemed intent on ripping the girl a new one.

Dragonslayer screamed into emergency war power in response.

The Executioner's stomach dropped as Grimaldi hauled back on the stick and the helicopter went nose vertical. The Sudanese jet streaked past underneath. The Stony Man pilot shoved the stick forward and kicked the collective. Bolan swung on his chicken straps like a hammock in a gale and caught sight of the glowing red lanterns of the Su-25's twin Tumansky turbojets. He brought the minigun around and squeezed the trigger. The weapon's motor whined, and the six barrels spun in a blur. Bolan's own red laser lines scored the night, and he saw bullet strikes sparkle on the Frogfoot's fuselage. The minigun could fire up to 3,000 rounds a minute as the electric motor whirled its six barrels at dizzying speed. The problem was that the Executioner was firing .30-caliber rifle bullets, and the boys at the Sukhoi Design Bureau sheathed their attack planes in titanium.

The Su-25 was firing 30 mm cannon shells and just one would light up *Dragonslayer* like the Fourth of July.

For this particular mission, *Dragonslayer* was stripped to pass foreign inspection and speed; her mission was search and rescue. Bolan's gun station was a last-second add-on for hostile-landing-zone suppression.

They had never made it to the landing zone.

The Su-25 fighter pair had dropped out of the sky on them like God's wrath. Fortunately these Sudanese fighter pilots had no experience in dogfighting. The Sudanese air force had spent the past two decades mostly strafing defenseless villages and refugee camps. The lead Su-25 had made the lethal mistake of trying to go low and turn and burn with *Dragonslayer*. Grimaldi had simply spun the chopper on its axis and given Bolan a lane of fire. The Executioner had ripped about three hundred rounds right up the Frogfoot's port-side air intake and put paid to the Sudanese pilot's account.

Wingman wasn't having it.

He had intuited the situation. His plane could approach six hundred miles per hour. His 1990s vintage Russian Doppler radar was a joke, but helicopters weren't exactly stealthy. *Dragonslayer* was a nice vibrating blob on his screen and the sun was coming up. The Su-25 was twice as fast than his prey and taking advantage of that fact. The Frogfoot pilot was climbing high and then screaming down for gun runs and zooming away before Bolan's ineffectual return fire could have any effect.

The soldier watched the Su-25 bank hard around in the purple light. "Jack, we're going to have to do this the hard way!"

"What are you suggesting!" Grimaldi shouted.

"Let's surrender!"

Bolan could almost hear Grimaldi smiling into his mike. "Okay! Let me see, Su-25, export version, his stalling speed has gotta be, what? Eighty-five? Ninety klicks per hour, give him a nice comfortable…"

Dragonslayer dropped altitude and noticeably began slowing as the pilot throttled back. The Su-25 continued its hard turn in the distance to come up on *Dragonslayer*'s six again. Sunlight began to pour over the Nuba Mountains to the east. Grimaldi held the aircraft in suicidal-level flight as he continued to drop speed. Bolan had a nice visual on the Frogfoot as it began to close.

"You want me to turn belly-up, as well?"

"No! But let's lose the ordnance!"

"Right!"

Grimaldi flipped a switch and the explosive bolts holding the M-134 on its mounts snapped like firecrackers. He tipped *Dragonslayer* just slightly to be helpful, and Bolan shoved the minigun out the door. The soldier hoped the enemy pilot was paying attention. Grimaldi held *Dragonslayer* steady at six hundred feet and 150 miles per hour. Bolan leaned back in his straps and lodged himself behind the cabin door frame. He reached back and slid his hand around the grips of his grenade launcher.

Bolan waited for the Russian 30 mm gun to blow him and Grimaldi to hell.

Even over the thunder of *Dragonslayer*'s rotors he heard the roar of the twin jet engines. The Frogfoot attack fighter pulled up alongside *Dragonslayer* like a traffic cop pulling over a vehicular offender. Morning light continued to spill over the mountains, and Bolan could see the Su-25 pilot pointing at Grimaldi and then pointing down at the ground.

The Stony Man pilot was waving back and grinning in a friendly fashion.

Bolan swung out on his straps. The M-32 Multiple Grenade Launcher was a 6-shot weapon. The soldier put the reflex sight slightly in front of the Su-25's port-side air intake and fired. The fragmentation grenade hit the Su-25 wing about six feet back and detonated harmlessly. Bolan dragged his sights forward to increase his lead and fired again. His second frag grenade detonated against the pilot's armored cockpit glass. Its only effect was to make the man nearly jump out of his seat. Bolan split the distance as the pilot yanked on his stick and fired the launcher four times in rapid succession. The soldier had front-loaded the M-32 with four frag grenades followed by an antiarmor round and white phosphorus.

The third frag missed.

His fourth bomb, the antiarmor and the incendiary grenades arced in the flight and were sucked up by the turbojet one-two-three like golf balls being eaten by a wet-dry vacuum. The Su-25 pilot had the unwitting decency to dive for the deck and take *Dragonslayer* out of collateral-damage range. Bolan had seen more explosions in his life than most men had had hot dinners. His eyebrows rose slightly as the Frogfoot shot a fifty-yard tongue of white fire from its port-engine nacelle.

Seconds later the Sukhoi disappeared as 3,000 liters of jet fuel came into violent contact with superheated gas, molten metal and a cloud of burning white phosphorus expanding in her belly to fill every internal crevice. Bolan watched as a ball of orange fire and white-and-black smoke fell from the sky like a slow-motion meteor. Bits of jetfighter with less drag fell from the fiery mass in little smoldering black streamers.

"Gosh…" Grimaldi observed. "Nice shot."

"Thanks." Bolan leaned back in his strap, broke open the smoking grenade launcher and reloaded. "I don't suppose we have a fix on our target anymore."

"No." Grimaldi sighed. "We lost our window. We're going to have to wait until target reestablishes contact."

Bolan snapped his weapon shut on a loaded round. Odds were they weren't going to get too many more chances. "Take us home."

"Copy that."

The Executioner glanced backward and watched the molten mess that had once been an airplane become a smoking hole in the dust of the Sudan.

All of this begged the question of just how exactly two Su-25s had gotten the jump on them. The Sudanese air-defense grid wasn't exactly state-of-the-art. Grimaldi had flown them in out of Uganda well under their 1980s vintage Soviet radars. For that matter, *Dragonslayer* had the most sophisticated electronics suite of any helicopter in existence. If the Sudan had been hammering the sky with their radar, Grimaldi would have known it. They hadn't detected anything until the Su-25 duo had suddenly swooped out of nowhere. Bolan and Grimaldi had been caught flatfooted. There was really only one explanation and it wasn't a happy one.

Someone had tipped off the authorities.

Lokichogio Airport, Lokichogio, Kenya

GRIMALDI WAS INCENSED. "Okay, someone tattled!"

Bolan pulled a sweating brown bottle of Tusker lager out of the ice chest and wiped it across his own sweating brow. The U.S. Military General Purpose Tent didn't have climate control. He cracked the bottle and shrugged. "Wasn't me."

"Somebody did."

"You checked her for bugs?"

The pilot scowled. He had gone over every inch of the aircraft before takeoff and triple checked after the Sudanese dogfight debacle. "Nah, you're right, I should have thought of that."

Bolan tapped the sat-phone icon on his tablet. He had already given Aaron "the Bear" Kurtzman a debriefing and was hoping for some follow-up.

"Bear, what have you got for me?"

Kurtzman came on the line instantly from the Computer Room at Stony Man Farm, Virginia. "Not much. That was a very interesting story you told me. I'd have to say the most interesting development is that there have been no new developments."

"No reaction from the Sudanese?"

"Not a peep. Nothing about unauthorized incursions into their airspace, much less any fuss about losing two of their attack fighters."

"So the question is, who knew about us?"

"Someone tattled!" Grimaldi muttered.

Kurtzman had clearly heard the pilot. "Striker, unless you think Farm security has been compromised, I'm putting tattling on the low-order-of-probability list."

"Then we were spotted, raised red flags, and someone put the tell-tale on us," Grimaldi stated.

"That's the way I see it, too, but I'm finding it kind of hard to fathom. Did you check *Dragonslayer* for bugs?"

Grimaldi reddened. You didn't see the man lose his cool very often. However, the Stony Man pilot was nearly always the ambusher rather than the ambushee. He had flown into suicidal situations and threaded the eye of the needle more times than Bolan could count. Getting ghosted and jumped out of the blue, or in this case the black, was an infrequent and unwelcome experience. Grimaldi glared at Bolan and raised his hands heavenward.

"Copy that, Bear," Bolan acknowledged.

"Then let's break it down. Who would have noticed you?"

Bolan grabbed his tablet and his beer, and stepped outside the tent. Grimaldi followed. Lokichogio Airport was a small facility and also extremely busy. It had become a hub for international and private aid and mercy missions in heartbreaking numbers. A small city of tents, container-unit shelters and prefabs littered the grounds around the main airport. Bolan and Grimaldi were posing as a private courier operation for a Farm-fabricated non-governmental organization, or NGO. The tent they had brought with them. *Dragonslayer*'s landing pad was a mostly level square of ground that someone had packed down with a lawn roller. Amenities were few. Bolan wanted to stay out of town, but the ad hoc city of aid workers was serviced morning, noon and night by roach coaches and street hawkers of all descriptions.

The fact was, between the humanitarian crises in the Congo, South Sudan, Darfur, as well as Ethiopia and Somalia, dozens of nations and NGOs were in a constant flux of representation. With that many interests, and that much money and aid flying in from all over the world and flying out in all directions, the city had also become a hotbed of smuggling and international intrigue. Kurtzman was right. Bolan's two-man team and *Dragonslayer* had attracted attention. They had barely been in Kenya more than forty-eight hours and had hoped to be out in the morning, long before any interest they attracted could materialize into anything.

The next question was how had they been tracked.

Anyone stupid enough to walk up to *Dragonslayer* to try to put a GPS tracking device on her would have set off her security suite, incurring Bolan's and Grimaldi's immediate wrath. Assuming someone with ninja-quality skills had succeeded, Grimaldi's pre- and postflight electronic security sweeps would have detected any invading electronic device.

Bolan considered how he would have done it.

"Bear, can you get me some satellite imaging?"

"What are you looking for?"

"I want some high-magnification infrared on *Dragonslayer,*" Bolan replied.

"Well…" Kurtzman considered the weird request. "She isn't moving, is she?"

"No."

"Well, what I'm most likely to see is a pair of glowing exhausts."

"Run a full infrared spectrum analysis," Bolan ordered.

"Okay…that's going to take a few minutes."

"Fast-track it if you can."

"All right." Far off in Virginia, Kurtzman clicked keys and made the magic happen. "The Pentagon has two birds that have a window on your position. You officially have high priority, but it's going to take a few moments to receive the command codes. Hold on. Syncing in your tablet…"

Bolan's tablet peeped at him and he touched an icon. The farthest flung, northwest corner of Kenya appeared in infinite shades of gray. The view plunged down through the atmosphere as the satellite locked on to his signal and began increasing its magnification. The haphazard mess that was Lokichogio resolved into a city and then an airport. Suddenly, Bolan found himself with a top-down view of *Dragonslayer.*

In the infrared imaging, her engine cowls still glowed a dull bone-white against the green-gray of the fuselage from the evening's earlier excursion.

"Tracking is locked and imager is calibrated, Striker. We looking for anything in particular?"

"Just a hunch. Let's start from the bottom and take it through the spectrum."

"That's not exactly this bird's job, but let's see what we can do. Starting at 0.7 micrometers."

A micrometer was one millionth of one meter, and it was often used in measuring infrared wavelengths. Point seven micrometers was the nominal edge of visible red light, and the spectrum extended out to 300. Such measurements went far beyond the ability of the human eye. *Dragonslayer*'s engines were one-offs, custom built specifically for a single aircraft, and powerful out of all proportion to her size. Like staring into the sun, most minor fluctuations in her infrared signature would be impossible for most instruments to detect. However, the right instrument using the proper filters could stare directly into the sun and detect heat variations all over the sun's surface as well as within it. Bolan was looking for a fluctuation that a high-intensity infrared imaging satellite, most likely a hostile one, would detect. Particularly a satellite that was on station, for that purpose, and that knew exactly what it was looking for and had a good idea where.

Bolan was looking for a cold spot.

The image of *Dragonslayer* slowly changed like a black-and-white photo polarizing. "There," Bolan said.

"I see it," Kurtzman acknowledged. "Increasing magnification."

The corner of Bolan's mouth quirked as his hunch was vindicated. The back slope of the main rotor housing was spackled with mysterious spatters of glittering white light.

"Man!" Grimaldi was incensed. "Someone done gone and gooed my girl! Rat...bastards!"

It was a trick Bolan himself had used. You could design chemicals to give off infrared light at specific wavelengths, suspend them in a clear, fast-drying gel and use them to mark objects or even people for unwitting targeting or tracing. If Bolan had to bet, someone had unloaded on *Dragonslayer* with a silenced, high-powered air rifle loaded with the equivalent of paint balls filled with infrared-emitting gel. It wasn't the sort of assault that would have triggered any of *Dragonslayer*'s security sensors, and if Bolan was the shooter he would have timed his shots to the nearly constant 24/7 roar of takeoffs and landings.

The soldier glanced over at the fuel truck and found his spackle-sniper's position. It was currently parked fifty yards away and serviced the helicopter park. Bolan looked out across the shelters and prefabs to the airport proper.

He had a very strong feeling he was under surveillance.

"Bear, I'm calling this mission FUBAR. We're marked and can't operate out of this theater."

"So the whole thing is a wash?"

"No—" Bolan stared northeast toward the cauldron that was the Sudan "—we're just going to have to do it the hard way."

"We're running out of time, Striker."

"You said Able and Phoenix are currently operating?"

"That is their status."

"I can't use blacksuits for this gig. I need mercs." Blacksuits were the military and police personnel who rotated onto the Farm to provide security duty for a period of time.

"Oh…my…God…"

"Find them for me, Bear. Break into databases and find me some reliable men."

"I don't know if I can get that authorized by—"

"Don't authorize it. Just do it."

"And to finance and equip this little jaunt I am…" Kurtzman's voice trailed off.

"I'm going to give you a password and an account number and authorize your access to an account a friend opened for me in Labuan. I had to stash away someone's ill-gotten gains."

Kurtzman paused a moment. "In Malaysia."

"Yeah. Malaysia."

"What will you need?" Kurtzman asked.

"About a squad, a lean one. Like I said, I want you to hack the databases, deal with each individual directly."

"Anything specific you're looking for?"

Bolan considered the Sudan again. "Any experience in the desert is good. Some French or Arabic is a plus, so would being able to ride a horse."

"What's the pitch?"

"I'll make the pitch. You offer them a first-class round-trip ticket and ten thousand euros to hear me out."

"Some of them might think its some kind of trap. I think you need to give me a little more."

"All right, we'll lead with the truth. Tell them it's a rescue mission that's probably suicide, and tell them to meet me in Chad." Bolan smiled tiredly. "Then let's see who comes."

2

CIA safehouse, Abeche, Chad

Bolan regarded the files in front of him. He had turned his back on whatever flapping and squawking was going on in Washington and charted his own course. He now found himself in Chad. He trusted Kurtzman and the Stony Man cyberteam implicitly, but privately even Bolan had been forced to wonder what kind of men would fly halfway around the world on twenty-four hours' notice to hear a suicide proposition in Chad. Bolan had his answer, and he had his men.

And his woman.

Kurtzman spoke from four thousand miles away over the tablet's sat link. "So what do you think?"

Bolan swiped his finger across the tablet and flipped the files back to the beginning. He had been expecting to see mostly Americans. Bolan looked at the sole Yankee on his team. Yankee was a loose term. Corporal Alejandro "Sancho" Ochoa wasn't exactly a Yankee. In his mug shot, the corporal was built like the light-middleweight boxer he had been. The tattoo of an outrageously buxom Latina in a sombrero and peasant dress covered his right arm from shoulder to elbow. A similarly shaped woman dressed like an Aztec priestess covered his left. An Aztec pyramid with the sun rising behind it covered his abdomen from belt line to sternum. Above that, San Jose 408 designated his hometown in California and its area code across his pecs.

Ochoa was grinning and throwing gang signs at the photographer. The only thing even vaguely military about the man was his high and tight haircut. Bolan shook his head. The jailhouse mug shot was hard to reconcile with the Army file photo of a grimly determined young corporal in dress uniform with the ranger tab on his shoulder.

"What happened?"

"It's hushed up, but basically his unit was involved in a bad civilian casualty situation in Iraq. He was individually cleared, but…"

"But his unit was made an example of. I remember something about it."

"His unit was sent home, then he had some brushes with the law," Kurtzman stated.

"Tell me he wasn't dishonorably discharged."

"Corporal Ochoa was given the opportunity to take an early discharge rather than face trial. He took it."

"And?" Bolan prompted.

"Our boy turns right around, joins Blackwater as a private contractor and heads right back to Iraq. He distinguishes himself and—"

"And Blackwater gets thrown out of Iraq for a civilian massacre."

"So Sancho went south and was doing bodyguard work in Central America, and, can you guess?" Kurtzman asked.

"He shot some people he shouldn't have."

"Well, rumor is they needed shooting, and rumor is a cartel down there wants him dead. Regardless, his privileges below the Rio Grande have been revoked."

"What's he up to now?"

"He's eking out living as a bounty hunter in the L.A. Latino community. His name is in every private security database in the U.S., but his record and his brushes with the law have him kind of blackballed."

Bolan sighed.

"You gave me forty-eight hours and some very interesting recruitment parameters, Striker."

Things looked a little better with the next two. Both men were

South African National Defense Force, 44th Parachute Regiment, Pathfinder Platoon and had made warrant officer. The pair currently worked for Transvaal Security Incorporated. TS Inc. provided security for African VIPs and were widely reputed to have supplied mercs during the Diamond Wars. The similarities ended when you looked at the picture of the two grinning men arm in arm holding up steins of beer. Gus Pienaar looked like a 1980s vintage Clint Eastwood with a mild case of albinism. Tlou Tshabalala bore a disturbing resemblance to a young Bill Cosby except with a shaved head and shrapnel scars on his left cheek and neck.

Bolan blinked at their bios. "They both married the other one's sister?"

"So it seems."

"Well, racial harmony is a good thing." Bolan had fought alongside and against South African mercs. They just didn't come much tougher.

He glanced over the recruit that came straight out of left field. Togsbayar Lkhümbengarav was Mongolian. It was a little known fact that Mongolia was a nearly constant provider of forces to United Nations peacekeeping missions. Sergeant Lkhümbengarav had been serving nearly continuously from Kosovo to Afghanistan. The previous year he had been right there in Chad. His specialty was a small arms instructor for indigenous peoples forming their own security forces. "Definitely keeping him."

"Thought you'd say that."

Bolan examined the one commissioned officer in the group, 1st Lieutenant Tien Ching from Taiwan. He had been a demolition man in the 101st Reconnaissance Battalion, better known as the Sea Dragon Frogmen. He had transferred to the 871 Special Operations Group and twice gone to the United States to cross-train with the Navy SEALs. He held numerous Republic of China army medals and citations but nearly all of his deployment records were redacted. "Anything else on Ching?"

"Just that the rumor that he has engaged in some very black operations in Mainland China. Then he went private in Japan. He seemed eager for work outside of Asia when we contacted him. I think the PRC may know who he is and is gunning for him."

Bolan dragged his finger across the screen and flipped open the next file.

Colour Sergeant Scott Ceallach had been one of Her Majesty's Royal Marines of 3 Commando Brigade. His individual formation in the Royal Marines had the name 30 Commando Information Exploitation Group. That meant the colour sergeant's job was to move ahead of the main marine force and find out information about the enemy, by fair means or foul, and exploit it as imaginatively as possible. It seemed he'd done some exploiting in Afghanistan before he had gone private.

"You like him?" Kurtzman asked.

"Royal Marine. What's not to like?"

Bolan looked wonderingly at the absolute wild card of the bunch, and askance at the baggage she had brought with her.

Elodie-Rousseau Nelsonne had been an agent for the French General Directorate for External Security, Action Division. Female DGSE agent spoke volumes.

"You sure about this, Bear?"

"I know, Action Division has a cowboy reputation, but you know what else they're also famous for?" Kurtzman queried.

Bolan did. "International rescues."

"That's right, and I have it on very high authority she's been involved in some of their more recent high-profile success stories, as well as some that never made the papers. She's been in Africa, and is currently doing work with Groupe Belge de Tour."

Belgian Tower Group was one of the premier European private contractors. That said a lot about Mademoiselle Nelsonne, as well.

Nelsonne had drafted two men of her own choice to fill out the squad. Valeri Onopkov was Russian and Radomir Mrda was a Serb. According to Nelsonne, both men were veterans in their own lands and had seen service in Africa. To Bolan that meant the wars in Chechnya and Bosnia respectively, and Russians and Serbians serving in Africa usually meant war crimes that could appall even the native militias that considered atrocity a national sport.

The phrase "beggars can't be choosers" came to mind. Bolan was running out of time and running out of options, and Kurtzman had delivered. Counting himself, it was a lean squad, and along with the target, if *Dragonslayer* was stripped for transport and they stacked everyone like cordwood, Grimaldi just might be able to extract them.

"What's the team's status?"

"We tried to make their flights coincide. No one has been waiting at the airport more than four hours. Ochoa's ETA is fifteen minutes from now. Then the shuttle will pick them up as a unit and bring them to the safehouse."

"I'll put out the welcome mat."

BOLAN AND GRIMALDI STOOD on the inner upstairs balcony of the safehouse and watched the team file inside. The house followed the general urban geometry of the Sahel and consisted of an almost featureless, two-story brown cube. The thick clay walls insulated against the heat of the day and the often bitter cold of the night. Being a CIA establishment, Uncle Sam in his mercy had installed air-conditioning. The climate control hit the mercs coming in off the street like a hammer, and they gasped and shuddered like people who had just plunged into an unheated pool. Bolan hoped no one had a heart attack. Abeche was in the running for the hottest major city on Earth. Three hundred and thirty-six days a year it was always over 90 degrees Fahrenheit. This day it was 115.

Scott Ceallach dropped his bags and tilted his head back in near ecstasy. He was a big, sleepy-eyed man. The Brit had grown a short mustache and beard since the photo Bolan had seen. He opened his eyes and looked up at the big American. His cockney accent was thick enough to cut with an ax. "Have a pint about?"

"Lager or stout?"

Ceallach raised his hand. "Bloody hell, squire, forget the sales pitch, I'm all in."

Ochoa grinned up, as well. The sport coat and mock turtleneck he wore hid his tattoos and his high and tight was freshly buzzed. "Yeah, me, too. Whatever it is, I'm down with it."

Bolan was pretty sure Ceallach was joking. Ochoa seemed in earnest. Lkhümbengarav and Ching were glancing around and talking to each other in low-voiced Mandarin. Lkhümbengarav looked nothing like his military photo. He had grown his hair out so that it could be pulled into a short ponytail, and he was cultivating a Fu Manchu mustache. If you closed your eyes and thought "Mongol," you would most likely picture Lkhümbengarav in a fur hat on a horse. He noticed Bolan's gaze and gave back a grin and a head bob. Ching regarded Bolan in open scrutiny but inclined his head.

Pienaar and Tshabalala stood as a unit.

"Lager," Pienaar stated. His accent told Bolan he was a South African of English descent.

Tshabalala grinned. "Stout for me."

Bolan examined former DGSE agent Nelsonne, and the woman regarded him back. She had an aquiline nose, widely spaced eyes, a generous mouth and a firm chin. Along with Tshabalala she was the only one who hadn't sweated through her clothes already. If someone had told Bolan she was a French movie star he would have believed it. Grimaldi clearly liked what he saw. She quirked an eyebrow at Bolan. *"Bonjour!"*

"Bonjour," Bolan replied. Onopkov and Mrda flanked Nelsonne like bodyguards. They looked to be very hard men. The Russian was tall enough to look Bolan in the eye but lanky to the point of looking cadaverous. Pale eyes measured the soldier out of slightly sunken sockets that seemed to have permanent dark circles. The Serb was a head shorter and built like a fire hydrant. His flat-topped brown hair stood up out of his head like nerve endings.

One look told Bolan that Nelsonne and her entourage had somehow acquired sidearms after landing.

"Leave your bags." He jerked his head. "C'mon up."

Grimaldi opened a tote bag as they filed up the stairs. "Phones and all electronic devices."

This was met with some grumbling, but phones, tablets, laptops and other devices were handed over.

The largest space upstairs had been converted into a conference room. Two folding tables had been pushed together, and ten chairs surrounded it. Bolan took the seat at the head of the table. Nelsonne took the foot and her two recruits flanked her. Everyone else filled in the sides. Without being prompted, servers entered, bringing roasted lamb, couscous, kebabs of vegetables and buckets of beer.

"That's the ticket!" Ceallach announced, and immediately began tucking in. The rest of the team attacked the spread like a wolf pack. Bolan waited until the first plate and the first beers had been consumed. He glanced behind him and a server brought in a covered dish. It was uncovered with a flourish to reveal banded stacks of euros.

Eating and drinking around the table ceased.

Five thousand euros had been wired to each individual when they accepted their plane ticket. The other half had been promised on arrival. Bolan took a bundle and tossed it at Lkhümbengarav. The Mongol grinned and snatched it out of the air. Bolan tossed bundles of cash around the table like a cash machine with a throwing arm. Mercs grinned and riffled the stacks.

"May I have your attention?"

Ceallach cracked open a Heineken beer and grinned. "All ears, guv."

"We're going into the Sudan, and the Sudanese government won't be pleased if we are discovered. We aren't officially sanctioned by any government. No one will come to save our asses if we get in trouble."

"Where in the Sudan?" Ching asked.

"Can't tell you."

That was met by a genuinely inscrutable look.

Tshabalala cocked his head. "What's the objective?"

"Can't tell you just yet."

The majority of the faces around the table went flat. Pienaar scratched his thin platinum hair and spoke for everyone. "So, we're just supposed to follow who knows who to who knows where to do who knows what? Sounds like shit to me, china."

"Sounds like *kak*," Tshabalala agreed.

Bolan shrugged. "Finish your beer, finish your food, take your money and walk."

Lkhümbengarav turned his gaze on Bolan. "Okay, GI, you saying I can drink my fill, eat my fill, take this money and go home? Five thousand euros?"

"At this point it's ten, but yeah."

"Round eye?" The Mongolian snorted. "You fascinate me. Uncle Sam just tossing his money away these days?"

"It's not Uncle Sam's money. It's mine, and I want you all in or on your way. It's going to get rough and mean really fast."

Nelsonne laced her fingers together and made a hammock for her chin. She smiled demurely. "Why all the secrecy?"

"We already made one attempt on the target. We got compromised and got jumped by Sudanese fighters."

"Sudanese fighters?" The Serbian spoke for the first time.

"A pair of Su-25s."

The Russian's eyes locked on Bolan. "And?"

"We shot them down."

Nelsonne kept smiling. "I have heard nothing about this."

Bolan nodded. "Yeah, funny about that."

Ochoa leaned back in his chair. "*Jefe,* I don't care if we're marching to Mars. I need the job. Ten thousands euros is a nice fat chunk of change, but you can't retire on it or start over. I've got no prospects and I got *mi madre* and nine brothers and sisters who really need a cash infusion. What's the pay?"

"Fifty thousand euros or its equivalent in any currency you want wired to the accounts I set up for you as soon as we deploy." Every face around the table save Grimaldi's and Nelsonne's went flat again. "Fifty thousand more to anyone who makes it out alive, success or failure."

Jaws dropped.

"Any medical care needed afterward will be fully paid at my expense. If for some reason there are delays or we need to extract and redeploy, I'm willing to entertain bonus pay."

You could have heard a pin drop.

Bolan shot a killer grin. "Who's in?"

Pienaar whistled and stared down the neck of his beer. "Tentatively, china, but what's the plan?"

"We're going to deploy on the ground posing as an NGO humanitarian convoy and then take a very unexpected turn."

Tshabalala visibly relaxed as he saw it. "And when we get close to the package we go low in the bush and acquire the package."

"That's about the size of it."

The Russian lit a contemplative cigarette. "And we drive back?"

"Maybe." Bolan nodded at Grimaldi. "Or he extracts us."

"And if there are more Sukhois?"

Grimaldi sipped his beer nonchalantly. "We already shot down two."

Bolan cracked himself another beer. "So, who's in?"

Ochoa shot his hand up. "Me!"

"Sounds like a bloody movie." Ceallach shook his head and raised his hand. "I'm in."

"Sounds like shit," Pienaar said.

"Sounds like *kak*," Tshabalala agreed.

The two men grinned and spoke in unison. "We're in."

Ching finished his beer. "Well, I have never been to the Sudan, and I have no pressing engagements."

Lkhümbengarav inclined his beer at Ching. "What he said, hot rod."

Bolan looked at Nelsonne, who reached for another beer. "I was already decided in Bruges."

Bolan didn't bother to ask the Russian or the Serb. He was pretty sure Nelsonne had decided them in Bruges, as well. "All right, real quick. We can all get to know one another later, but our mission language is going to be English, and I need to keep things simple." Bolan looked at Tlou Tshabalala. "You got a lot of la-la-las for tactical communications."

"Call me T-Lo, everyone does."

"Done."

Gus Pienaar piped up without being asked. "Goose, been my name since I was kid."

Bolan looked at his Royal Marine. "Ceallach?"

Scott Ceallach rolled his eyes and put the "lock" in Ceallach. "Cee-a-laaahckh."

"How about we just call you Scotty?" Bolan suggested.

"And I've been living with you Yanks' *Star Trek* fetish all my life, haven't I, then? And I'm not even Scottish!"

"Good to know." Bolan glanced at the Mongolian. "Luck-um-ben…?"

The former sergeant smiled like he'd seen it coming from a long way off. "Been 'Lucky' on the last three UN deployments, GI."

Tien Ching raised his beer at Bolan. "T.C."

Valeri Onopkov nodded at Bolan. "Val."

Radomir Mrda grunted. "Rad."

Bolan perked an eyebrow at Nelsonne. *"Mademoiselle?"*

She nodded. "Russo."

Ochoa frowned. "Aren't you going to ask me?"

"Ask you what, Sancho?"

"Hey! How did you— Oh, man, never mind, and what do we call you, *Jefe?*" Ochoa looked at Ceallach. "Squire?"

"You can call me Striker."

Nelsonne made an amused noise. *"Très Américain."*

"I am that," Bolan admitted. "Last question. Who besides me can drive a Unimog?"

"Me," Pienaar replied.

"We have two Land Rovers. Who's volunteering to drive?"

Mrda and Lkhümbengarav raised their hands.

"Good enough. Everyone finish eating. Take a nap. I've got nine beds set up. We're leaving at sunset."

The team resumed tucking in. Nelsonne hadn't taken her eyes off Bolan, and she was still smiling. There was a saying in the United States spook community that there was no such thing as an ex-CIA agent. Until they buried you, you were just on standby.

Bolan was pretty sure there was no such thing as ex-DGSE in France, either.

3

"I believe they call this flying by the seat of your pants," Grimaldi said.

"That's your job," Bolan replied.

Bolan and the Stony Man pilot sat in the conference room comparing notes. The team had collapsed in their beds with mild heatstroke and food comas. Grimaldi gave his old friend an amused look. "I mean, did you actually look at these yahoos?"

"I'll admit Sancho is a little squirrelly."

"No, big guy, Sancho's the only one I trust." Grimaldi frowned. "Except for maybe the Brixton Bomber and the Mongolian, and the South Africans are okay, except every time I see them I hear the song "Ebony and Ivory" in my head, oh, and T.C. He seems like a stone-cold killer of men."

That was two-thirds of the squad. "So...you don't like Russo?" Bolan asked.

"Oh, I like her a lot, but she makes me nervous, and so do those ex-Communist-bloc savages she has with her."

Bolan controlled his bemusement. "Bear picked her."

Grimaldi made a noise.

"How we doing on gear?"

"I've got a Hercules on the airstrip with all three vehicles and all requested equipment stowed and ready to go. I'll get you and the team on the ground and in the saddle. After that it's up to you."

"Thanks, Jack."

The pilot shifted in his seat uneasily. "This is messed up. I should be going with you. I should be driving."

Bolan kept his poker face. It was an interesting phenomenon that pilots automatically assumed they were NASCAR drivers in the making. In Bolan's experience, "knight of the air" and "rubber meets the road" were two different sciences entirely and rarely mixed well. "I need you hot on the pad, Jack. Ready for extraction from a hot LZ at heartbeat's notice."

"Well, if you put it that way," the pilot said, "I'll drop you off and be waiting by the phone."

Both men turned at a polite knock. "Come in," Bolan said.

Nelsonne walked in smiling, went to the sideboard and made herself a whiskey and soda. "I have taken the liberty of acquiring us a pair of guides."

Bolan regarded the French agent drily. "Where will they be guiding us to?"

"That is up to you, but they are men of Central Sudan, and have acted as guides and interpreters before. I think you will find them useful in a myriad of ways."

"You vouch for them?"

"I have worked with them. They are good men."

"Where are they?"

"Waiting outside." Nelsonne batted her lashes at Bolan. "Would you like to meet them?"

"Well, it's awfully hot outside for standing around." Bolan leaned back and pressed the intercom button. "Two guests outside. Show them up."

In moments two men in their early twenties appeared in the conference-room doorway and looked in shyly. Both were as tall as Bolan but stick-thin. Their skin was so black it almost seemed blueish. That told Bolan the two men were at least by blood from the South Sudan. Despite the heat they wore matching blue jeans, denim jackets and cowboy boots. They had identical huge brown eyes and even huger identical smiles.

"They are twins," Nelsonne explained.

"Let me introduce Haitham and Shartai Kong."

Bolan gestured for his guests to take a seat. "You gentlemen hungry?"

The Kong brothers nodded and sat.

"You guys drink beer?" the soldier asked.

"Yes."

Bolan hit the intercom for the kitchen. "Could we get a pitcher of beer and some of that lamb up here for our new guests?" Bolan leaned back in his chair. "Kong…that's a Dinka name."

The brothers nodded, their shy smiles becoming slightly prideful.

"From Kurdufan?"

Kurdufan was smack-dab in the middle of what had once been the Sudan, and like the Sudan itself Kurdufan had been split into north and south. It was a bit of luck because that was exactly where Bolan was going. The Kong brothers nodded in proud unison.

"Mademoiselle Nelsonne says you're both excellent guides."

Bolan was fairly certain it was Haitham who answered. He had a Darth Vader–quality baritone. "Guides, interpreters." He gave Bolan a sly smile. "Scouts."

Bolan smiled back in suspicion. "SPLA?"

The Sudanese People's Liberation Army had been fighting the government in Khartoum since the mid-1980s. Haitham's chest swelled as he stood and pulled up his T-shirt to show a puckered bullet scar in his lower right abdomen. Both Bolan and Grimaldi's eyebrows rose as Shartai stood, turned, unbuckled his pants and dropped his trousers to display a long pink scar creasing one buttock. Shartai slapped it for emphasis. Both men burst out laughing and sat again. "Since we were children."

Bolan glanced at Grimaldi.

"They have a good attitude," the pilot admitted.

One of the staff brought in a mound of leftover sliced lamb on a bed of couscous and a pitcher of beer. The Kong brothers tucked into the food and greedily began sucking down beer. That told Bolan they were either Christians or animists. The fighting had driven untold numbers of Dinkas south as they had battled the government of the Muslim-dominated North. Christians were ruthlessly suppressed. The traditional African spiritualists were often annihilated out of hand. Nelsonne swirled the ice in her drink. "I have told them you pay well."

Neither man stopped eating but their eyes snapped to Bolan as they kept shoveling it down. Bolan saw no need to be stingy and he wanted their absolute loyalty, and to him rather than Nelsonne.

"Let's keep it simple. I've already hired nine team members. I see no reason to treat you any differently. As full members of the team I'll give you ten thousand euros now as a signing bonus, and…"

The Kong brothers stopped chewing and food nearly fell out of their mouths as their jaws dropped.

"And fifty thousand more on completion, or to your families if you're killed."

Haitham wiped his chin with the back of his fist and leaned back. "You are serious?"

Bolan went to the safe in the wall, punched in his code and produced two bundles of euros. He sat back down and slid them across the table. "I'm deadly serious. This is going to be hazardous duty, and that's why I'm paying hazardous-duty pay. I think the two of you will be invaluable members of my team. You in?"

"Oh, indeed," Haitham said.

"Most assuredly!" Shartai was in full support.

Bolan raised his beer. "Welcome to the team. Jack?"

Grimaldi finished his beer. He knew what was coming. "Yeah?"

"Go get the plane ready."

Darfur

VEHICLES ROLLED FROM the belly of the C-130. The two Land Rovers were loaded with crates, and the canvas-covered load in the Unimog concealed just under half a ton of fuel, supplies and ordnance. Everything was marked as humanitarian aid. The 4x4s were painted the same beige as the dust storm that was kicking up. The jump-off was auspicious. With a storm coming the landing strip was abandoned. Lkhümbengarav backed a Land Rover down the ramp. "Sancho! Scotty! You're with me," Bolan shouted over the wind. "And Lucky, you're in Rover 1!"

Haitham shouted through the *shemagh* covering his face. "I am with you, boss!"

"Hop in!"

Everyone except Bolan grabbed his or her bags and clambered aboard.

Bolan made the backing out motion with his hands. "Bring it out, Goose!" The Unimog truck rolled out under Pienaar's guidance. Tshabalala was already riding shotgun. An MZ 125 SX off-road motorcycle was mounted on brackets on the front and rear bumpers.

Bolan waved the last vehicle out. "Rad! Rover 2!"

The Land Rover whined in reverse as the Serb extricated the vehicle. Nelsonne and Onopkov jumped in as a unit. Shartai shouted out of his scarf-swaddled face, "Boss! With permission? I will go with the *mademoiselle!*"

"Go!"

Shartai clambered in to Rover 2. Bolan squinted into the wind and dust behind them and clicked the tactical clipped to his shoulder. "All units, hold up. We have company."

Two vehicles were heading in their direction.

Bolan raised his binoculars and examined the vehicles. One was a Chinese-made military 4x4 and the other a flatbed truck. The back of the truck contained nine men in camo. They all carried Kalashnikovs and their faces were swaddled against the dust. Bolan squinted at the dust-covered windshield of the 4x4. The man in the passenger was wearing mirrored blue sunglasses and a black beret. Nelsonne appeared at Bolan's side with Mrda and Onopkov in formation behind her. Bolan handed over the optics. "Any idea?"

"I believe it is Captain Osman Osmani."

"You know this jack wagon?"

Nelsonne handed back the binoculars. "I do not know what a *jack wagon* is, but I strongly suspect that he is one."

"So this is a shakedown?"

"Most likely. However, he is not some greedy, sitting-on-his-hands captain who just accepts bribes. He was very active in the fighting both in Darfur and South Sudan. It is very likely the United Nations will get around to trying him for war crimes. The information I have is that he has actually stepped up his strong-arming and extortion to build up his nest egg before he flees prosecution."

Grimaldi spoke across the com link. "You want me to take off?"

"No, that'll just make the captain suspicious. Come on out. Leave the ramp down, but be ready on my signal." Bolan watched the vehicles approach. "Everyone out. Be friendly. Remember, we're an NGO helping displaced refugees. I'm going to try to pay these guys and send them on their way. But be ready to take them down. Follow my lead."

The rest of the team formed up. Ochoa took position at Bolan's right hand. "Hey, *Jefe?*"

"Yeah, Sancho."

"You said take these guys on your go?"

"That's right."

"These guys got AKs. I can see them from here."

"It does appear that way."

"Yeah, but, you haven't given us any guns."

Lkhümbengarav nodded. "What he said, hot rod."

"We're in an international group of doctors, drivers and volunteers. Osmani and his men don't expect resistance. If it comes to it, we jump the sons of bitches, pound them like nails, confiscate their weapons and disable their vehicles."

Ceallach cracked his knuckles with an explosive ripple of pops and cracks. "Right! The old-fashioned way, then." He raised his hand and waved at the approaching vehicles in a happy fashion. One of the gunmen in the back of the flatbed actually waved back. The vehicles ground to a halt. The soldiers jumped down out of the flatbed, some with their rifles in hand. Others had them slung. Most had their folding stocks folded. They were in a low state of alert. The captain was more leisurely as he let his driver jump out and open the door for him. Two soldiers got out of the back. The officer wore a stainless-steel Ruger .357 Magnum revolver in a conspicuous gunfighter's rig low on his thigh.

Bolan arranged his face into an obsequious smile and stuck out his hand. "Good morning…" He made a show of looking at the patch on the man's shoulder and smiling hopefully. "Captain? I'm Dr. Cooper."

Osmani barely acknowledged Bolan's guess with a slight nod. He ignored the outstretched hand. The big American looked at his hand and lowered it sheepishly. The captain had the accent of a man whose primary language was Arabic. "I am Captain Osmani. I will see your manifest immediately."

Bolan blinked in feigned surprise. "We already passed customs and inspections in the capital. Is there some kind of—"

"Your manifest, Dr. Cooper. Immediately."

Bolan nodded at Grimaldi, who held out his clipboard. Osmani's driver intercepted the clipboard and then handed it to his captain. Osmani flipped through the pages listing medicines, medical equipment, water purification gear and various aid-station necessities.

"Captain," Bolan said, "I'm very sorry you had to come out in the middle of this storm." Osmani inclined his head and gazed at Bolan over the rims of his sunglasses like a snake eyeing a not particularly fast or wily insect.

Bolan recoiled and let himself stumble on over his words. "I mean, Captain, as you may have heard, there has been an outbreak of dysentery in the interior. We need to get our water-purification equipment on-site as quickly as possible. Every second counts." He stammered like a man who wasn't used to these sorts of negotiations. "Is there any way we could…" Bolan made a show of swallowing a frog in his throat. "Expedite things?"

Osmani handed the manifest back to his driver, who handed it back to Grimaldi. The captain lowered his official hostility by a tiny increment. "I am aware of the ongoing humanitarian crisis. Rather than requiring you and your people to return to the capital and—"

Nelsonne gasped on cue and clutched Bolan's arm. "Return? But, no! We bring—"

Osmani didn't miss a beat. "But it would be better for you to continue your humanitarian mission immediately. However, since I have been dispatched in my official capacity, certain permits will have to be authorized."

Bolan looked at the captain like a deer in the headlights. "I understand completely. I was given some money for…discretionary expenses."

"Excellent."

"How much do you…?"

Osmani sighed tolerantly. "How much discretionary income do you have?"

Bolan very reluctantly produced a money belt from under his shirt.

Osmani's driver leaned in and whispered something in Arabic. Both men looked at the Kong brothers. The driver whispered urgently. Osmani went reptilian once more. "Who are these men?"

"They are Abdullah and Salva. Interpreters recommended by the Red Cross in Nyala," Bolan explained.

"I am reminded of a story about a pair of twins I have heard. Rebels and war criminals who are wanted in Khartoum."

"Captain, I assure you—"

"I am taking these two men into custody. You will submit to a full inspection of your cargo. You will mount your team into your vehicles and return with me to town where the matter will be investigated further. Your passports and all currency both foreign and domestic will be temporarily held. You will button up the plane, leave it here and the pilot will come along, as well."

Bolan let his jaw drop and made a show of failing to draw up some dignity. "Uh…team? This must be some kind of mistake. We'll get it cleared up back in town. In the meantime, I want you to obey the captain's every order and assist him and his men in all ways." Bolan turned back unhappily. "Will that be sufficient?"

"For the moment."

"What would you like to inspect first?"

"You will show me—"

"This?" Bolan's sucker punch snapped the bridge of Osmani's sunglasses and the septum beneath. The right uppercut lifted Osmani onto his toes and sat him down. Pienaar and Tshabalala exploded into synchronized flying rugby tackles that pushed two of the men holding their rifles into the dust. Bolan spun 360 degrees and his spinning back-fist clouted Osmani's driver like a ball and chain. Nelsonne's leg flew upward in a goose step from hell and her savate kick toppled a man, spitting teeth as he fell to the ground. Bolan looked for his next opponent.

His team had the situation well in hand.

The Executioner turned his head just in time to see Tien Ching relax his hands. Three men lay fallen at his feet in moaning ruin. Ochoa stood over a man who clutched his groin and vomited. Mrda had his man in a stranglehold and was easing him down to the ground. Onopkov rubbed his head and lit a cigarette. His man lay on the ground with an egg-size lump between his rolling eyes. The Kong brothers gleefully stomped the truck driver who lay in a ball trying to cover himself.

Bolan watched with admiration as Ceallach pressed his opponent over his head and hurled him against the grille of the truck. "That's for you, wee man!" he roared. Wee man bounced brutally off the bumper and fell fetal into the dust.

Bolan waved the Kong brothers off. "Enough."

Shartai gave the truck driver a last kick for good measure, then the brothers began walking up and down the line of violence, collecting weapons.

Bolan looked at Grimaldi. "Where were you?"

The pilot waggled the manifest. "Someone had to hold the clipboard."

"Thanks, Jack."

"No problem." The pilot looked meaningfully into the mounting storm. "Can I go now?"

"Yeah, you're out of here." Bolan turned to his team. "Haitham, Shartai, load their weapons into the back of our truck. Speaking of weapons, Lucky, break ours out. Goose, T-Lo, burn the command vehicle. Who here is good at tying up people?"

Nelsonne smiled winsomely. "I am quite talented at securing men."

Bolan grinned. He bet she was. "Secure the prisoners. Rad,

Val, help her and then load them in the back of the truck. Leave them any water they brought. Confiscate any phones or radios. Sancho, disable the truck engine, and I mean permanently, then help Scotty get the canvas top on over the prisoners. Once you've finished your jobs I want everyone to go to the Mog and Lucky will issue you weapons." Bolan watched as his team set about their tasks with well-oiled precision. "We're out of here in twenty."

4

The Sudan

The dust storm died at dusk. The team set up camp for the night in a dry creek bed and strung camouflage netting across the three vehicles to form a covered camp. It was a cold camp, as well. They kept no fire, and the heating elements of the MREs were used in the back of the truck. Bolan walked over to the Unimog. Nelsonne sat in the cab monitoring the radio. Everyone was bundled against the sudden chill. "Any chatter?"

"Nothing on the captain, but I suspect his superiors keep him on a loose leash. He has carte blanche to commit his crimes, and they demand their cut when he reports in. I don't think anyone will go out looking for him until tomorrow, perhaps the day next."

"You think he'll come after us?"

Nelsonne sighed. "You should have killed him."

"That would have drawn the wrong kind of attention. He was humiliated, and he's going to have to explain how he got his ass kicked to his superiors. I'm betting he won't. He's going to pay off whoever pulls him and his men out of that stalled truck. If he tries to come after us, it's going to be a private vendetta. I'd like to think I forestalled any official notice of our departure."

"You have a gorgeous mind." Nelsonne sighed again longingly. "I would still like to have seen you kill him."

"It may still come to that."

Ceallach appeared at the other cab door. He held a couple of steaming coffee mugs and passed them out. "Bit of all right this morning, then."

"Yeah, you gorilla-slamming one of Osmani's men was pretty impressive."

The Briton made a self-deprecating noise. "Call that a 'potato toss' back home."

Bolan knew Ceallach hadn't come to reminisce about the morning brawl. "What's on your mind, Scotty?"

"Been talk among the lads."

"What kind of talk?" Bolan prompted.

"Well, we're feeling a bit like mushrooms, then, aren't we?"

It was a mantra invented by U.S. Special Forces during the Vietnam War.

Mushrooms: kept in the dark and fed on shit.

Ceallach sipped coffee and turned a contemplative eye to the Sudanese night. "Well, you wouldn't hear me saying it…."

Bolan decided to give a little. "The target is a high-value individual, and may require forcible extraction out of a refugee situation."

Ceallach nodded knowingly. "You know, Striker? I've seen this movie. Wrong part of Africa, but in the end everyone dies but you and the sexy bird."

"I saw that movie, too." Bolan nodded. "Wasn't bad."

"Is there a sexy bird, then?" He gave Nelsonne a wink. "Besides the one we already brought along?"

"There is," Bolan stated. He slid out of the cab. "I'm going to check the perimeter."

"I'll stay here and guard Russo."

Nelsonne smirked.

Bolan scooped up his rifle.

Lkhümbengarav had issued weapons just before the convoy had headed out, and grumbling had ensued immediately. Ceallach went so far as to give it the raspberry. Bolan's team were all spec ops or at least elite-unit veterans. It had been some time since they had seen wood-and-gunmetal-blue weapons rather than black plastic and matte-black Parkerized steel. That wasn't quite true. They saw it often, but almost always in the hands of the hapless people opposing them.

The Chinese Type 81 rifle looked like a stretched version of an AK. The one nod to the twenty-first century was the forward-mounted optical sight that John "Cowboy" Kissinger, Stony Man Farm's armorer, had mounted where the rear iron sight used to have been. In its favor, the rifle could fire the ubiquitous Russian .30-caliber ammo littering the Sahel, it came equipped with rifle grenade-launching rings, and Bolan's team was currently dripping in them.

Mrda was on sentry duty. The Serb spoke quietly across the link. "Striker."

"Yeah, Rad?"

"Contact."

"All units, arm up. Prepare to break camp. Everyone get your night-vision eyes on. Drivers, get behind your wheels but do not start your engines. Sancho! Haitham! With me!"

Ochoa appeared at Bolan's elbow in an eyeblink. He had volunteered for the role of the soldier's right-hand man, unasked for but with admirable will. Haitham loped out of the darkness. "Striker-man!"

Bolan put a finger to his lips. Haitham fell into formation and the three warriors jogged toward Mrda's position. They stopped running and quietly climbed the ladderlike clay side of the arroyo. They stretched out on either side of Mrda. The Serb was staring intently through the scope of his Dragunov sniper rifle into the wasteland. "They're coming straight toward us, Striker."

Bolan brought up his binoculars.

It was a scene he had seen more times than he could count. The people walked and limped in a small mob. Everything they owned they carried. The lucky ones had blankets wrapped around them against the evening cold. There were far too many women, children and the elderly, and far too few men and boys. They hunched and searched the sky for the sound of jets or rotors. They cast fearful looks behind them for the terror that had driven them into the desert night. Bolan saw no weapons beyond walking sticks and crutches.

"Jesus," Ochoa muttered. "'Give me your tired, your poor, your huddled masses…'"

"'Yearning to breathe free,'" Bolan continued. "'The wretched refuse of your teeming shore. Send these, the homeless, tempest-tost to me, I lift my lamp beside the golden door.'"

Ochoa turned to Bolan. "Jesus, Striker! You gave me goose bumps!"

"You been to the Statue of Liberty, Sancho?"

"No." Ochoa grinned beneath his night-vision goggles. "But I've been to the Rio Grande."

Bolan snorted. "You'll do, Sancho." He clicked his com link. "Scotty, bring up the SAW. I also need a canteen of coffee. Put a lot of sugar and powdered cream in it."

"Roger that, Striker. On the double."

Mrda's sniper rifle never wavered from the refugees. "How do we play it?"

"Me, Sancho and Haitham are going to go talk to them. You and Scotty are going to cover us."

Ceallach trotted up the arroyo with his Type 81-1. It was simply a Type 81 assault rifle with a longer, heavier barrel, a bipod and a 75-round drum. The Briton handed Bolan the canteen, then snapped open the legs of the bipod and took position next to Mrda. "Bob's your uncle, Striker!"

Ochoa sighed. "I don't understand a word he says."

"Let's take a walk." Bolan walked out into the night flanked by Ochoa and Haitham. They covered about a hundred yards and stopped. Bolan watched the mob blindly approach through his night-vision goggles. At fifty yards he pushed up the device on top of his head and took a glow stick out of his web gear. He gave the stick a bend and a shake and a green glow filled the night. The platoon of refugees immediately came to a halt. Several individuals bolted from the group in random directions. Bolan stood with his rifle slung and waved in a friendly fashion. Haitham called out in Arabic. An old man and an old woman detached themselves from the group. Each wore a gray humanitarian-relief-issue blanket like a shawl and each leaned on a stick. The two came forward warily. The old man had an ancient-looking Sudanese arm dagger strapped just below his shoulder. Haitham nodded to the elderly couple and exchanged quiet words with them.

He turned to Bolan. "They are Sirel and Mina. They are Christians, and displaced farmers."

Bolan uncapped the canteen and held it out. Sirel caught the smell of coffee and insisted that Mina drink first. Sirel waved his arms and spoke rapidly. Haitham translated.

"They say bad men attacked their camp, though they got warning across the missionary radio and managed to leave. They fear the bad men are still looking for them."

Ochoa rolled his eyes. "What do they have that anyone would want?"

"Women," Bolan said. "And children. They're commodities around here."

Ochoa turned his head and spit. "Christ wept."

"Haitham," Bolan said, "ask them if it's Captain Osmani they're afraid of."

Mina spoke for the first time. She started speaking low, but she began waggling her stick and speaking in greater and greater outrage. "Mina says that Osmani is bad. Everyone knows who he is. He comes and he takes any gold or silver or medicine, but these men are worse. They come on horseback. They take everything, and they are led by a terrible individual called Yellow Mnan. They say he keeps hyenas in his main camp and feeds people to them." Haitham stopped translating. "Something about him being an…evil ghost?"

Bolan considered that. "Ask her if Mnan is black like you but has skin like me."

Mina nodded and made the sign against the evil eye.

"He's an albino." Bolan knew how much of a badass an albino had to be to rise to a position of leadership in a genocidal civil war.

Mina continued.

"Anything Mnan does not want, he burns," Haitham said. "Anyone Mnan does not want, he kills." He frowned. "And Mina says when they kill they take their time."

"Sound like some real loco hombres, *Jefe*," Ochoa added.

"Janjaweed," Bolan said.

Sirel and Mina flinched in unison.

Ochoa brightened. "Ganja weed?"

"Janjaweed, Sancho. It's an Islamist militia. They were originally drawn from the nomadic tribes in East Darfur. The Sudanese government used them to try to pacify the rebelling farming tribes who were mostly Christian and Native African animists. The lines got blurred pretty quickly. At one point it was rumored the government in Khartoum was emptying the prisons, giving each man a horse and an AK, saying, 'Go west, young man.' They were widely accused of genocide."

"Jesus…"

"Jesus is right, Sancho. They're real bad hombres, and loco." Bolan did a quick head count and clicked his com link. "Russo, I need thirty-seven protein bars and the same of the bottled waters."

"Sacre bleu!" The French agent sounded bemused. "Do I detect a big, fat heart in that American chest?"

"Just do it." He turned to Haitham. "Ask them how far behind Mnan and his Janjaweed men are."

Sirel spoke for long moments. Haitham looked as if he might cry. "Sirel says his people are the dead, walking in dust. They leave little to follow unless one of them dies. He says Mnan probably does not know where they are, but he will be roaming for his next prey."

"Jefe?" Sancho asked.

"Yeah?"

"I don't like this Mnan. I don't like him at all."

"Me, neither, Sancho."

Nelsonne walked up with Onopkov behind her. The lanky Russian carried a big box. The refugees were scared of Bolan and his group, but they recognized international aid immediately and swarmed forward for food and water. Nelsonne smiled, chucked chins and passed out food and water and hugs like a pro. More than the concentrated calories and desperately needed hydration, the woman was passing out empathy, and hope. She was also quickly interviewing each person she fed. The French agent was also cataloging interviews as she distributed aid. When the last elderly person had cracked the cap on his water bottle and the last child had crinkled open the wrapper of his food bar, Nelsonne rose and leaned in to Bolan. "Tell me."

"What?"

"Tell me we're going to wipe the Sudan with this Mnan."

"The French do have the term 'mission creep,' I assume?"

Bolan had to factor in the fact that Nelsonne was an intelligence agent and quite possibly had her own agenda, but the woman seemed to be getting genuinely worked up about the refugees. "Then why did we stop and give them food? We fatten them up for slaughter?"

"To get intel? Because we couldn't have them walk on top of us and set up camp?" Bolan suggested.

"We're going to kick Mnan's ass."

"We just might teach him not to go our way." Bolan watched the refugees as they finished their rations. They sat huddled together, literally leaning against one another to hold themselves up. Half had already fallen into exhausted sleep. Some couldn't help themselves and tore into the rations Nelsonne had issued for the morning. "Or theirs."

"So we kick his ass?"

Bolan considered the geometry of horror in sub-Saharan Africa. Sirel and Mina's people had left tracks. The only reason they hadn't been ridden down already was that Mnan and his cohorts had probably found something else to temporarily distract them. Sirel and Mina's little band had women worth raping and young girls to be sold in the slave trade. They also had young boys who could be used the same way or turned into child soldiers; and when all was said and done, Yellow Mnan would be very interested to hear about a heavily loaded convoy headed into the interior.

Bolan nodded. "We're going to kick him in the nuts and see how he likes it."

Nelsonne rose up on her toes and kissed Bolan on the cheek. He smiled as his right cheekbone tingled pleasingly. The soldier clicked his com link. "Lucky, put the Rovers into gun-jeep configuration and prep the cycles."

The Mongolian grinned. "You got it, hot rod."

Nelsonne stood on tiptoe and breathed in Bolan's ear. "Hey, soldier. You want to get laid?"

"In Bruges," Bolan murmured back. "And only if we win."

5

Bolan's caravan went hostile. By the dawn's early light, Rover 1 now sported a recoilless antitank gun mounted in the bed and an automatic grenade launcher on the hood for the man riding shotgun. Rover 2 mounted a Russian .50-caliber machine gun in the bed and a light machine gun in the passenger-side hood mount. The caravan's mother ship, the Unimog, had a ring-mounted .30-caliber gun on the cab roof. Each vehicle was packing a HongYing 5 shoulder-launched antiaircraft missile in the back, and had locked and loaded RPGs.

Pienaar lit a cigarette. "So, you and T-Lo going on recce?"

"If we're not back by noon, start heading east. We'll catch up. If you haven't heard from us by sunset, we bought it. In that event I gave Russo a number to call. You'll be informed of the mission parameters and asked if you want to continue. If the team agrees to go ahead, I want you to take command. Though I would pay particular attention to anything Russo has to say. The French have assets and intel in the region."

"Copy that, Striker." Tshabalala walked up and the two brothers-in-law fist bumped. Pienaar jerked his head at Bolan. "Have him home at a decent hour, T-Lo. Keep your hands to yourself."

Tshabalala threw back his head and laughed.

Bolan threw a leg over his bike. His MZ 125 SX motorcycle was German-made and ex-French military issue. The four-stroke thumper had been painted matte black and was remarkable for weighing only 124 kilos while at the same time being remarkably tough. Tshabalala checked his kit one more time and looked at Bolan expectantly. He had declared himself an "aces" cross-country cyclist. It turned out Pienaar was an actual local South African champion and had taught Tshabalala all he knew, but Pienaar was also the most experienced truck driver, as well, and had become Bolan's de facto second in command.

The Executioner pulled down his goggles and grinned at his companion. "Tshabalala?"

"Say it ten times fast, china."

Bolan gave the scout a sly look before he pulled down his goggles. "Zulu?"

Tshabalala grinned and pulled down his own. "Too right I'm Zulu."

"You're down with the plan?"

"Well, it sounds a bit like mission creep to me. Then again, this Mnan sounds like a real clutch plate."

Bolan kicked his MZ into life and headed out across the hostile landscape. Tshabalala took position at his eight o'clock.

By sunrise the Sudan was beautiful in its own harsh way, and one had to experience the African sky firsthand to understand all the talk about it. The soldier followed the path the refugees had left. The track was faint, and the morning wind was wiping out what there was, but they were made of up the very young and the very old without much in between. Guessing their route was simple enough.

It wasn't long before Bolan saw dust in the distance. Tshabalala spoke across the com link. "Contact, Striker!"

"I see it." Bolan spun his bike to a halt. If he could see the contact's dust, the contact could see the rooster tails Bolan and the Zulu's bikes were hurling up. "Let's set up shop."

Tshabalala brought his bike in front of Bolan's broadside-on, and the big American laid his bike down behind it. He unlimbered his rifle and his optics and laid himself out across the warm metal of his bike. Tshabalala hid his rifle behind his bike, pushed up his goggles and stood in plain sight as if he hadn't a care in the world; except that he might possibly be having motorcycle trouble. Bolan scanned the approaching dust cloud from behind his companion's front forks.

The only thing the horsemen were missing was a banner that read The Janjaweed Are Coming!

The word *Janjaweed* was an Arabic colloquialism. Taken in context it literally meant a man, with a gun, on a horse. Mnan's men qualified. The Janjaweed had gone from scrappy militias of Arabic nomadic herders who quarreled locally with the settled farmers over water and land resources since time out of mind, to well-equipped and organized cavalry cohorts that operated with overt support from the government in Khartoum, and often co-incided their raids on farming villages and towns with Sudanese military air strikes.

Fortune had turned once more.

South Sudan was working toward full independence and Dar-fur was heading in the same direction. Much of the Janjaweed's open support had dried up. Times were hard, but young men who had spent the past five to ten years raping and pillaging to their hearts' content weren't easily returned to the hardscrabble exis-tence of herding goats and camels on the Sudanese plains. The Sudan was full of refugee camps and villages struggling to re-build. The civil wars were nearly over, but there remained plenty of plunder for the hard-hearted.

The oncoming men looked like a hard-bitten bunch. Native dress and turbans supplemented their remaining bits of well-patched army camouflage. Gold and silver bangles and necklaces stolen from the dowries of assaulted village women gave the Jan-jaweed terrorists a piratical appearance. A horse fancier would find little to love about the narrow and poorly conformed local Dongola horses they rode. The breed made up for their ungainly appearance with the hardiness and stamina that anything that in-tended to survive in the Sudan required.

Tshabalala raised his *shemagh* and waved it happily at the horsemen. "I make it a reinforced scouting party, Striker. Prob-ably others out there looking to pick up the refugees' trail."

"I figure it the same."

The horsemen came boiling forward. Those who didn't already have their rifles in hand geared up. Some fired their guns in the air. Others pointed their weapons at Tshabalala and fired wild potshots and bursts from the saddle. He stood his ground.

As the range closed some rounds began cracking past a little too close for comfort. Tshabalala grabbed his rifle and dropped to a knee behind his bike. "Any requests, Striker?"

"Spare the horses. Don't start firing until they're within three hundred yards."

"Okay."

They waited. Tshabalala made a disgusted noise. "Oh, can you believe that?"

Bolan had never seen a man try to fire an RPG-7 from the back of a horse, but one of Mnan's men had that can-do attitude. The Janjaweed rocketeer struggled to control his galloping mount with his knees as he leveled his launch tube. "That's just wrong."

The rocket-propelled grenade thumped from its launcher and hissed across the plain. The outraged horse reared in shock and terror. The antitank grenade exploded about fifty yards wide into a rock formation. Bolan waited for the rearing horse to drop back to all fours, then shot the rocketeer out of the saddle.

Tshabalala sighed happily. "We…are…engaged." His rifle began cracking in slow methodical semiauto. "Cell phone!" he shouted.

The two warriors fired at the same time and the tattletale shouting into his cell phone rolled back off his horse's rump with the double hit. The remaining horsemen sawed savagely on their reins. Bolan swept his sight from target to target. Every time he dropped the hammer he dropped a horseman. The last Janjaweed terrorist stood in his stirrups defiantly and burned an entire AK magazine in Bolan and Tshabalala's general direction.

The Executioner rose as his companion's first bullet sat the man back in the saddle and his second knocked him out of it.

Tshabalala brought his smoking muzzle inches from his lips and blew on it. "Aces."

"Not bad," Bolan agreed. "You any good with horses?"

"I'm a fucking centaur, china."

"See if you can gather the horses up and string them. Police up any fallen weapons."

"Right, on it." A few of the horses had sprinted away. Most were huddling together shuddering and pawing the ground near their fallen riders. Tshabalala sauntered toward them casually making South African cowboy clicks and chook-chook noises. For shell-shocked horses from a breed with a notoriously high-strung and nasty disposition they responded remarkably well to the Zulu invader.

Bolan walked among the fallen.

The ComBloc 7.62 mm rifle cartridge was the ballistic equivalent of the old American cowboy rifle .30-30. A man who took a round in the center body mass rarely needed shooting a second time. Falling off a galloping horse afterward didn't help matters. Bolan gave the living water even as he opened his pack and began confiscating weapons, wealth and cell phones. Tshabalala came back with a string of eight horses and riding the lead. "How's the treasure and spoils?"

"We've got some pretty thin wads of Sudanese dinars, Egyptian pounds and Kenyan shillings. A pretty fair stack of gold and silver dowry bangles and necklaces." Bolan glanced up. "Why do you ask?"

"You're gonna give the horses, the money and the guns to Sirel and his people?"

"I was going to give it all to them."

"Don't mind so much." A pirate gleam came into T-Lo's eyes. "Wouldn't mind a dip into the gold pile. None of the lads would. Got a wife who might admire a bauble, a bangle or two."

"You remember Mina's granddaughter? The one you bounced on your knee this morning and gave a candy bar? You had Goose take a picture. Tell your wife you tore the baubles, bangles and beads right out of her hands."

"Now, that's rough talk, china."

"Those people have nothing, T-Lo. In this part of the world a dowry determines whether a woman gets a decent marriage or is virtually sold off as a slave. The women get the gold and silver. The men get the guns and the horses to keep it. Once I've gleaned any intelligence out of the cell phones, they get those, as well. It's not much, and someone may well rip it all right back out of their hands, but if they can get across the border it might just give them a fresh start, and if any of their young men are left, it's something to come home to."

"Aw, hell, Striker." Tshabalala rolled his eyes. "Didn't really mean it."

"Yeah, you did, but I knew the precious child of light inside you would see reason."

The Zulu snorted. "Well, can I be Santa Claus when we get back?"

Bolan tossed him the jingling pack. "Be my guest."

SIREL WEPT OPENLY AS HE pressed his forehead against Tshabalala's hands. He endlessly repeated two of the few English words he knew. "Thank you…thank you…thank you…" The Zulu's skin was dark like the refugees, and he spoke Arabic. He had played the roll of Santa Claus to a tee and Nelsonne and the Kong brothers had been his smiling helpers. The oldest and most infirm now sat upon horses. The Janjaweed's blankets, shelter halves, canteens and food supplemented the refugee band's meager supplies. All of the adults had a small roll of currency to call their own. The few old men who knew which end of a rifle was which, now had one. The mothers and matrons wore necklaces, and the little girls stopped just short of strutting as they showed off their new gold and silver bangles. Bolan had used his sat link to locate the nearest Christian missionary station. It was one hundred miles to the border, but Sirel seemed to know the plains.

Ochoa sighed at the scene. "You think they'll make it?"

"I'm willing to admit to a ray of hope." Bolan turned his gaze on Tshabalala. The Zulu merc felt Bolan's stare. "Aw, now, I already admitted you were right!"

Pienaar's head snapped around. "You tried to dip into the refugee fund, didn't you!"

"Well, I didn't, did I?"

Pienaar punched his brother-in-law in the shoulder. "Love him, but light fingers on this one!" The refugees didn't understand, but they laughed at the obvious tomfoolery. The Kong brothers took the map Bolan had drawn and began giving Sirel specific instructions and advice.

Ching walked up with an uncharacteristic smile. The Taiwanese operative held up one of the captured cell phones. "Clandestine does not exactly describe these men."

The number highlighted on the screen belonged to Commander Mnan.

"Not so much," Bolan agreed.

"I have determined that the owner of this phone is named Abdullah. Mnan has left a number of increasingly agitated text and voice messages. Abdullah must have been the squad leader."

"Good work, T.C." Bolan took the phone and connected it to his own. He pressed Mnan's preset number. The phone call was answered nearly instantly. Bolan held the device away from his head as a stream of angry Arabic spewed out of the receiver. The name Abdullah figured prominently in the dressing-down. Bolan's let his voice grow cold. "Abdullah's dead, Mnan. Speak English."

The voice on the other end of the line suddenly spoke with a surprisingly cultured English accent. "To whom am I speaking?"

"The man who has Abdullah's cell phone."

"I see."

"Do you?" Bolan countered.

"May I ask as to the status of my men?"

"Two were alive when I left them. They received remedial first aid and I left them with a canteen of water each, but they require immediate medical attention. I'll allow you to retrieve them."

"You are very kind. I gather the infidel farmer, Sirel, and his people are under your protection?"

"I will allow you to come south far enough to pick up your wounded. Afterward I recommend you head north and never enter this part of the Sudan again."

Mnan's voice turned sly. "And should I fail to take your advice, I gather you will not be responsible for what happens?"

"I will be directly responsible for the death of you and every one of your men."

Mnan's side of the line was quiet for a moment. "Did you know that when I stake a man out naked for the hyenas, they always go for the genitalia first?"

"Good to know."

"I look forward to making your acquaintance," Mnan said.

"I'll kill you as cleanly as circumstances permit." Bolan clicked off and tapped the app for Home. "Bear, you got that?"

"Got him," Kurtzman replied. A satellite shot with gradients appeared on Bolan's screen. A dot appeared to the north. "He's calling from about a hundred klicks northwest of your position. I'm training a high-resolution imaging satellite on him now, give me a few seconds."

"What have you got on Yellow Mnan?"

"Nothing good. He's almost a Sudanese urban legend. Some sources say he doesn't exist. It seems like the UN and African Union forces don't believe he exists because they just don't want to. It's too embarrassing, and too horrifying. His depredations over the past ten years are reputed to have ranged from an arc all along the Darfur border, taking a nice long dip into the South Sudan and then back again. One reason no one can confirm his existence is that he doesn't leave survivors. Anyone he does leave alive is sold in the human trafficking market and is off the grid. With South Sudan and Darfur turning into prototype states and foreign aid pouring in, he's had to bring his troop back into Sudan proper. But there are so many refugees heading south and west out of the Sudan his pickings are still pretty good, and if he doesn't have Khartoum's tacit approval I'm a monkey's uncle."

Kurtzman's estimation jibed with Bolan's. "Request *Dragonslayer,* air strike, on Mnan's position."

The computer expert made an unhappy noise. "I'll put in the request. Don't hold your breath. As of now, *Dragonslayer* has permission for just one more task in the Sudan, and that is extraction."

Bolan had figured as much. "Keep me posted."

"Copy that," Kurtzman replied. "You really going to send Sirel and his people limping south by themselves?"

"What else would you have me do? Take them with me?"

"No. You know what I mean."

"I do," Bolan stated.

"You have a mission to the east. Sirel and his people are heading south, and it sounds like this Mnan has a real hard-on for them. I can't help but worry about those people."

"There's all kinds of trouble between Sirel's people and the South Sudan, but you don't have to worry about them and Mnan."

"Why is that?" Kurtzman asked.

"Because now Mnan has a hard-on for me."

6

Captain Osmani glared into the mirror at the tape covering his broken and flattened nose. His broken upper-left incisor throbbed abominably. He thrust a cotton rag dipped in oil of clove against it and wished to the nine hells he hadn't sold off his medic's supply of morphine for cash. He resisted the desire to reach into the desk drawer and take another slug of French brandy. He had already drank a third of the bottle.

Osmani's driver and adjutant, Kiir, limped into the tent. The left side of his face was lumped and swollen from Bolan's backfist. Osmani snarled. "What!"

"You have a visitor, Captain!"

"Who even knows I am here! Who could—"

The visitor broke protocol by showing himself in. Osmani's face flushed and it made his tooth hurt worse. The man was Chinese. Despite the heat and dust, the intruder's tropical-weight, English-cut, French blue suit was immaculate. His suit and his haircut bespoke the legion of Chinese businessmen and diplomats infesting Khartoum. To Osmani, the way the man carried himself clearly said *soldier.* "Good afternoon, Captain Osmani," the man said in faintly accented English. "My name is Rao Kai Rong."

Some choice words in rejoinder occurred to Osmani. Instead he reexamined the man in front of him. It was well known that Chinese visitors were held in high esteem in Khartoum. In return for raw materials and oil, the PRC was pouring millions of yuans into the Sudan in the way of financial aid, military equipment and assistance in infrastructure development. From the government in Khartoum down to the local magistrates, everyone was privately dipping into this river of money. Osmani himself was a beneficiary of this largesse. Like most Sudanese military men, the captain at least privately objected to the army of Asian invaders who felt they could come and go as they pleased without so much as a by-your-leave. Osmani's first and second assessments agreed.

This Chinese was dangerous.

Osmani arranged a smile on his mangled face. "What is it I can do for you?"

"Perhaps it is more of a question of what I can do for you, Captain."

"How pleasing. In what endeavor would you like to assist me?"

"I understand you have had an incursion," Rao said.

"What leads you to this…understanding?"

Rao gave Osmani's face a sympathetic look. "In fact it is only conjecture, perhaps I am ill-informed."

Osmani glowered.

"Allow me to introduce a hypothetical, Captain. If indeed you were to have had, shall we say, an altercation, one in which you had been set upon in a cowardly fashión by foreign invaders, but during the altercation you had been in an unofficial capacity? You might be loath to report it. Particularly in the case that you had been defeated and had lost significant weapons and matériel."

Captain Osmani considered the Helwan pistol on his hip. It angered him further that the weapon was a battered reserve pistol. The American had taken Osmani's prized, personal .357 Magnum revolver. He decided not to shoot the Chinese just yet. "And, so?"

"And so weapons and matériel are easily replaced. Information, on the other hand, is priceless."

"Information always has its price."

Rao allowed himself a smile. "We understand each other exactly."

It occurred to Osmani that one or more of his men had been talking. "What do you suggest?"

"Could you describe the men who so treacherously attacked you?" the Chinese asked.

At the moment Osmani saw little reason to lie. It was obvious Rao knew of the situation. The question was how to profit from it. Osmani decided to put some cards on the table. "I believe two were local. Wanted war criminals and twins from the Kurdusfan. It was when I attempted to take them into custody that they suddenly attacked."

"The two Sudanese, were they the Kong brothers?" Rao asked.

Osmani's eyes widened momentarily. "So I believe."

"Who else?"

"They were men of many nations, passing themselves off as an international NGO. There was a woman—I believe she was French—and a black man, but I did not hear him speak. The rest were Caucasians, Europeans or Americans, except two who were Asian."

"Asians? Interesting. Can you describe them?"

"One was Chinese, like you. He annihilated three of my men, with his hands and feet."

"Interesting. The other?"

"The other was different."

Rao cocked his head. "Japanese? Thai?"

"I would not know the difference, but he was shorter than the Chinese I have met, but compact, powerful." Osmani put his fingers to the corner of his eyes and pulled them up into thin slants. "His eyes were like this, very—"

"Mongolian?" Rao offered.

Osmani released his face. "Yes, that would describe them, and him. Mongolian-looking."

"Interesting. Tell me about their leader."

"Big. American, by his accent." Osmani nearly flinched as he remembered the heartbeat in time that the flustered, bumbling American doctor had blurred into a bone-crushing whirlwind. "Cold eyes, blue."

"A squad of foreign soldiers, mercenaries, posing as aid workers on Sudanese soil. Clever enough to arrange the situation so that you would be unlikely to report them, whether they succeeded in bribing you or defeated you."

Osmani's fingers itched for his gun. "So it would seem."

"If you concur, I would like to leave the incident unreported."

"To be quite honest, Mr. Rao, I am considering killing you so that the incident remains unreported." Behind Rao, Corporal Kiir's hand went to the butt of his pistol.

Rao seemed unconcerned. "If you were to do that, it would leave me unable to help recompense you for your lost weapons and vehicles. It would also leave me unable to help you quietly take revenge upon those who have insulted you and the Sudan People's Armed Forces, as well as leave me unable to offer you extremely lucrative compensation for any aid that you render me in this…mutual situation."

"Please, forgive my being forward, but how is this situation mutual?" Osmani queried.

"A team of foreign mercenaries, posing as aid workers, has invaded your country. Has it occurred to you to wonder what exactly is it that they want?"

Osmani's lip curled. "To fight for the rebels."

"The rebels are rather poor, and if they were to spend the money, would they not prefer crates of Kalashnikovs, RPG-7s and shoulder-fired surface-to-air missiles as opposed to a handful of men, however skillful?"

"They are military advisers, hired by the oil companies who want a free, non-Muslim South Sudan that is friendly to the west."

"A better guess, but why are they entering Kurdufan? The oil is farther south. Why spear inward into the heart of the Sudan itself? Their pretense of being NGO workers has already been shattered yet they continue eastward away from safety in Darfur."

Osmani considered that. His pain, the brandy and, to his chagrin, shame at his defeat had kept him from thinking about it clearly. "They want something."

"I believe so."

"What?"

"What if were to tell you that your lost weapons and vehicles will be replaced, indeed, you will be given ones of much higher value and they will be expanded to equip, say, a platoon of your picked men? All of your men will be highly paid in cash. You, your second in command and your staff will be given private bank accounts with large sums in them. During our excursion into the interior, any and all plunder and spoils will be yours. Equipment, gear, vehicles, weapons and monies we take from the mercenaries are yours, as well."

"Very generous. What is it that you shall be taking from this endeavor?"

"I ask only the right of first interrogation against any of the mercenaries, particularly their leader. When I have determined they are of no further use to me, you may take whatever vengeance you wish upon them or ransom any of them if you see fit."

"I see." Osmani saw that despite the seeming generosity of the terms and assistance he was very likely getting the short end, and a very short end, of the stick. "Information is priceless."

"Indeed it is. For example, consider the value of information circulated in Khartoum, that Captain Osman Osmani is regarded with great fondness by certain allies of the Sudan. How might that affect his military career? Indeed, what if certain allies of the Sudan insisted that in security matters, military exchange, training exercises and arms sales on dealing specifically with General Osman Osmani?"

"General." Osmani spoke the word before he could stop himself.

"Should foolish bureaucrats in Belgium wish to try to bring charges against such a dear friend and ally, would it not be useful to have friends in the General Assembly, indeed, the Security Council who would vouch for him, much less veto the attempt and strike his name from the rolls?"

Osmani tried to control his face. He had spent the morning debating his options for bolting the Sudan. Suddenly his prospects expanded into the horizon.

"I will further give you my word, Captain, that the information I seek, if it is indeed what is suspected, would be of absolutely no use to you. Indeed, if you were to possess it, it would most likely get you killed. It is the sort of information that takes the government of a world power to absorb, conceal and act upon."

Osmani wrapped his mind around that. This was obviously an intelligence operation of some kind.

"This is the extent of my offer," Rao concluded. "If we have an agreement, I hope you will allow me a small team of my own men."

"I have no pressing engagements, and you may bring whomever you see fit. How soon do you wish to leave?"

"Shall we say in the morning? In the meantime, would you allow me the honor of sending a man to look at your tooth?"

Osmani tried to keep the sudden rush of eagerness out of his voice. "That would be kind of you."

"Very well, I will look forward to seeing you in the morning." People's Liberation Army of China Non-Commissioned Officer Level 6th Rao walked out of the tent, then shook his head. Like all creatures not born to the Middle Kingdom, Captain Osmani wore his heart on his sleeve and his thoughts on his face. Given the situation this was extremely useful, and given the situation a man like Osmani was exactly the correct tool. Rao hadn't even had to lie. If Osmani proved as useful as Rao thought, the captain might indeed make general and be exactly the kind of toady Beijing would want in Khartoum.

Rao took out his phone and punched in a code. He spoke to the robot operator defending the communications link. "This is Rao, Operation Dragon Fire is go."

South Kurdufan

"TWO MEN?" YELLOW MNAN stood over his fallen man as he turned his mirrored gaze on the small sea of dead men. The jackals had run off at the approach of Mnan's forces. On the other hand there were no braver vultures than those of the great plains of the Sudan. The scavenger birds had eyed Mnan and his horsemen and technicals warily, then continued feasting. "On motorcycles?"

Harun looked up at his commander through a haze of pain and fear. Mnan wasn't physically imposing, but he *was* scary. He was gaunt to the point of emaciation, and his French jungle fatigues hung from his bones as if they were on a clothes rack. His features were Dinka, and by Dinka standards he would have been a remarkably ugly man no matter what the color of his skin.

In direct sunlight his skin was a blotchy, whitish yellow. One hardly ever saw Mnan's skin in direct sunlight. Day or night he wore a wide black cowboy hat that kept his face in shadow. Day or night he work black gloves and French mountaineering sunglasses. If he had any attractive feature it was his hair. His albinism had given him hair color of corn silk. Mnan's women took great pains to flatiron and relax it for him, and the American General George Armstrong Custer would have admired the way Mnan's blond hair spilled in curls out from under a cowboy hat.

"At first we thought it was a lone man. Some fool. Easy pickings. The other had laid his motorcycle down, like a horse, behind him. They had rifles with scopes. It was an ambush."

Mnan squatted on his haunches and adjusted his Uzi on its sling. "Describe them."

"One was an American. The other was a black. From the south."

"South Sudan?"

"South Africa. I recognized his accent from the movies."

"I see." Mnan smiled kindly. "How do you feel, Harun?"

Harun had a pair of bullet holes in his chest that somehow had managed to miss his heart and lungs. "It hurts, Commander."

Mnan reached into his pocket and pulled out a morphine auto injector. Harun sighed happily as warm, syrupy goodness filled his veins and eclipsed his pain. "You fought well. You will be avenged."

"Commander, I—" Harun's eyes rolled as Mnan gave him a second ampoule. Mnan pushed the selector switch on his Uzi to semiauto. Mnan's second in command watched from his imposing height. Makur was just under seven feet tall. "You are merciful, Commander."

"Mercy for my warriors," Mnan intoned. "None for our enemies. Are we assembled?"

Makur extended a huge spatulate hand at the assembled technicals. The nine Toyota and Ford 4x4s all had the roofs of their cabs cut off and light and heavy support weapons mounted in their truck beds. "Your technicals sped to you as soon as you called. Two broke down on the way but only need minor repairs.

The horsemen follow as quickly as they can without killing their mounts."

Mnan pressed the muzzle of his Uzi to Harun's temple. Harun's eyes continued to roll. Mnan's Uzi cracked once and Harun collapsed like a boned fish. "These mercenaries." Makur scowled. "Whom do they fight for?"

"They are not mercenaries." Mnan rose. "They are adventurers, and their adventure in my Sudan will end in horror." Mnan's head snapped around. "You brought my babies?"

Again Makur stretched a huge hand. One of the pickups contained four 2XL dog kennels bolted to the bed rather than support weapons. Mnan smiled and whistled. The alpha bitch of Mnan's personal troop of hyenas chuckled at him and her three littermates cackled in response. Most Africans from Tripoli to Durban considered hyenas extremely dangerous vermin. While hyenas resembled dogs, they were actually more related to cats, but like dogs, they were eminently trainable, and by a strange twist of the Holy Koran, Mnan thought, unlike dogs, they were not considered unclean. He strode toward a technical with quad-mounted antiaircraft guns. "Makur, my brother. Let us go meet the American."

7

Kurdufan

"Technicals," Kurtzman said. "On your trail, armed and driving hard. It's a pretty good bet they belong to Mnan."

Bolan rode shotgun in Rover 1 with Lkhümbengarav and Ceallach. It had been a lovely afternoon jaunt across the Sudan until now. "How many?"

"Nine, and there are horsemen about forty klicks behind them."

"How many?"

"Resolution is difficult with the bird I have on line, Striker, but I'm guessing about sixty."

Lkhümbengarav shook his head. "Shit."

"Bear, can you get me resolution on the technicals? What kind of firepower are they mounting?"

"Resolution isn't what it could be, Striker. Looks mostly like support weapons, but having spent the time working for you that I have? One looks like a flatbed with a quad-mounted AZP-23 installation."

"Bloody hell!" Ceallach snarled. "That outranges everything we have!"

The Russian 23 mm autocannons were designed for air-to-air combat between jet fighters and low-level surface-to-air defense, and had an effective range in the ground mount of two and a half kilometers. One would be bad enough. In a quad mount it would chew any vehicle in the caravan to pieces with one burst. Bolan's

Land Rovers and bikes could race ahead and escape the modified civilian vehicles with ease, and leave the horses foaming and shuddering in their dust. The Unimog was the mitigating factor. It could do distance about as well as a Russian half-ton, and Mnan would use that to leapfrog his lighter vehicles ahead to pin the convoy down and bring up his big guns to finish them off.

Bolan rose in his seat and clicked his com link as he cut his hand in a circle overhead. "Convoy! Full stop!"

The Unimog and Rover 2 ground to a halt. Tshabalala was riding ahead and he spun his bike around. Bolan's team spilled out of their vehicles for a conference.

"Listen, Mnan didn't take the hint, but it looks like he took the bait. He's coming after us," the Executioner stated.

"With bloody antiaircraft guns, Striker!" Ceallach angrily reiterated. "Our 87 mm is the biggest thing we've got, and you'll be lucky to get any accuracy at all beyond five hundred meters! Mnan's 23s can shoot a bloody English mile, then, can't they!"

Ceallach waved his arms at the brown, Martian-looking landscape. "And I don't see much in the way of bloody cover, either, Striker!"

Bolan turned his attention on the Briton. "Are you done now?"

Ceallach recoiled slightly under the soldier's cobalt gaze. "Well…yes."

"Good. Scotty's right. We've got nothing to match up to an AZP, and we have to plan on them having half a dozen heavy machine guns and RPGs. We're outnumbered, outgunned and outranged."

Nelsonne gave Bolan a sunny, expectant smile. "So what do you propose?"

Bolan had been thinking about that. "Simple."

"What have you got, hot rod?" Lkhümbengarav asked. "You ain't shooting horsemen out of the saddles on this one."

"Good point. So we're going to use the same ambush but reverse the tactics. T-Lo and I took Mnan's cavalry out at range because we had rifles with optics and they didn't."

Ochoa's brow furrowed. "So you're going to reverse it by…?"

"We're going to ambush Mnan's technicals at close range."

Onopkov chain-lit another cigarette and did some math. "Nine of them. Three of us. We ambush them at close range?"

"Yeah."

Nelsonne just kept smiling. "How do we do that?"

Bolan pulled a shovel out of the brackets on the Rover 1's tailgate. "We dig."

West Kurdufan

CAPTAIN OSMANI LAUGHED out loud. Rao nodded. "You are pleased?"

Osmani watched the Liebao, or Cheetah, commander vehicles roll up outside his tent in a convoy. To the untrained eye the vehicles looked like Mitsubishi Pajero SUVs. The trained eye would notice the cargo racks on the hood, the roof and the back-bed doors. Beneath the luggage racks on the roof the military man would notice highly modified central sunroofs with ring mounts for weapons. Behind the Cheetahs a pair of Chinese NJ2046 high-mobility 4x4 trucks pulled up the rear.

What pleased Osmani the most was the vehicles' white paint and the large UN letters emblazoned on the sides and hoods. "I am well pleased, Mr. Rao."

"Did I mention that once this operation is over my superiors would like you to accept these vehicles as token of their respect?"

Captain Osmani just barely kept the surge of cupidity off his face. "That is very kind."

The driver's doors of the six vehicles flung open simultaneously. The drivers all wore khaki cargo pants and vests and matching sunglasses. They stepped up to Osmani and Rao in formation and saluted smartly. Their leader barked out in English for Osmani's benefit, "Tsu, reporting as ordered! All equipment and personnel present and accounted for!"

"Very good, Tsu. Captain, my men do not speak Arabic, but all are fluent in English. I propose we keep this our communications language."

"Very well."

"Would you like my men to drive for yours? Or would you prefer to designate your own drivers?"

Osmani suspected all of Rao's men spoke Arabic fluently, and that these men would be keeping tabs on the conversational trends of each of Osmani's fire teams and reporting directly to Rao in Mandarin. "Your drivers are more familiar with the vehicles."

"Very good." Rao motioned to one of the truck drivers. "Ting, break out the weapons."

Osmani leaned over and whispered to Corporal Kiir in the language of his birth. "Kiir, spread the word. If our men need to communicate anything among themselves or to me that the Chinese should not hear, speak in Beja."

"Yes, Captain."

Rao's men went to one of the trucks and began unloading wooden crates. Tsu and Ting came back with a crate between them and opened it in front of Osmani. The Kalashnikov was the worldwide symbol of the freedom fighter, the revolutionary, the terrorist and Third World armies who belonged to the spray-and-pray school of marksmanship. Colt's M-16 rifle was the penultimate symbol of the American soldier. The Americans had spent the past four decades kicking the living hell out of any and all that opposed them. Any derivation of the M-16, particularly the M-4 carbine, was a highly prized status symbol.

Osmani reached into the crate and pulled out a Colt carbine. Despite the lack of markings or serial numbers on the weapon, he suspected it was a product of Norinco Industries. The weapon mounted an optical sight on the top rail.

Rao nodded. "The reflex sight is instinctive, however, with your permission I would like my men to give yours the weapon's basic manual of arms immediately and a few hundreds rounds of practice fire."

"I concur." Osmani looked up at the sun. "How far behind the invaders do you believe we are?"

"According to my last intelligence report, we are approximately three days behind them."

Osmani frowned. "I saw their vehicles. They have Land Rovers and a Unimog. Your vehicles are slightly more modern, but do you truly believe we can catch them?"

"My men have night-vision equipment. Where the terrain is safe we will drive at night. That should help make up time." Rao gave Osmani a smile that was genuinely inscrutable. "And should it become necessary, I believe I have the means to delay them."

GOOSE AND TSHABALALA rode back on the cycles. There was no place to hide the Unimog, and it was too big to bury. Bolan had ordered the South Africans to drive it out of visual range and to return on the bikes. It rankled everyone to leave the truck and the overwhelming majority of their supplies unattended, but it was better than having their matériel blown to smithereens.

The South Africans brought their bikes to a halt in front of Bolan. Pienaar pulled down his goggles and grinned at the excavations and field fortifications. "We miss anything, Striker?"

Ceallach leaned on his shovel and spit to one side. "Just the bloody hard bits, mate."

Bolan examined his two main fighting positions. Central Kurdufan wasn't quite a Martian landscape. In fact it looked a lot like the bastard lovechild of the Australian Outback and one of the harsher corners of Texas. Bolan had taken a dried riverbed and dug himself two very quick and dirty revetments fifty yards apart. Rover 1 and 2 were hidden from sight, but when the enemy came down their trail they could move up the dirt ramps just enough to expose their weapons; and if they were taking heavy fire they could roll back down. Both Ochoa and Ceallach new their way around a recoilless antitank gun. The Briton would be loading and Ochoa firing. Haitham would be in the driver's seat either bringing Rover 1 up or down the revetment. Shartai would be driving Rover 2, and Onopkov would be firing and Nelsonne assisting on the Russian .50-caliber gun.

If the enemy had mortars of any size, the revetments would be about as useful as sand castles at high tide.

That brought the second half of the plan to bear. The gun jeeps were going to be the knockout punch. It was going to be the men in the fighting holes a hundred yards ahead who were going to be lead blow. Ching and Lkhümbengarav would be in one hole. Tshabalala and Pienaar another. Bolan had a hide directly behind a pile of tombstone-size rocks to himself. Mrda was off to one side at two hundred yards with his Dragunov.

Bolan gazed eastward across the empty terrain toward the Unimog's position. He tapped his phone. "How close are they, Bear?"

"By last estimate they should closing, Striker," Kurtzman replied. "Twenty minutes to visual if they are making time as of last sat window."

Bolan nodded at Pienaar. "Pop smoke."

The South African hit his remote detonator. Out by the Unimog a white phosphorus grenade detonated. The team watched and waited. A plume of smoke rising in the distance rewarded them. That was the bait. Mnan and his men would see the smoke on the horizon and head straight for it and right into the jaws of the trap.

Bolan went over the plan one more time. "We left a nice trail for Mnan and his men to follow. With any luck they're going to come straight down it. You all wait on my move. Once me, T.C. and Lucky, and T-Lo and Goose are engaged, Haitham and Shartai will bring the Rovers to the lip of the revetment and Rover teams engage with the support weapons. We need to make this quick."

Mrda lit a final cigarette before battle. "And I?"

"Wait for the first bullet or explosion. After that, no one will spot you off to the side except by sheer dumb luck. Fire at will, but focus on the weapons operators on the technicals rather than the drivers or gunmen."

"Okay."

"Any questions?"

Ceallach raised his hand.

"Scotty?"

"Yeah, not to be dick, Striker, but what about that bloody quad-mounted 23?"

"We're currently out of satellite window. I don't know whether it's still with the main force or if the lighter technicals are jumping ahead. If it makes an appearance, drop down. Both you and Rover 2. My hope is that they come rolling in and Rad shoots the operators and we take that flatbed at will. If it's hanging back, we wipe out the main force and the entire team retreats to the riverbed and see what kind of move he makes. If he wants to sit back and think he has us pinned down while the horse cavalry catches up, we let him, and when night falls we creep in and take him. If he wants to take to his heels instead, we'll let him do that, too. Anything else?"

Bolan looked around at his team. No one looked particularly nervous or displeased with the plan. Haitham and Shartai looked positively giddy. As far as the Kong brothers were concerned, greasing the Janjaweed was a mission perk. Bolan nodded. "Rad, you're our spotter. You let me know when they're within a hundred yards of the ground teams."

"Okay."

Bolan took up his weapon and fighting vest. "Let's do this." His gun crews broke for the Land Rovers. Ching and Lkhümbengarav and Pienaar and Tshabalala broke off into their fighting pairs and moved out into the scrub toward their prepared pits. Mrda jogged off to snipe from the flank. Bolan walked to his lone fighting position at the tip of the spear. His crown of rocks was large enough to crouch behind, but he had dug himself a shallow grave in case Mnan sent scouts ahead. He had inundated a blanket with the red dust of the Sudan and stretched it between tent poles. A cursory glance would show nothing but a patch of dirt.

Bolan shoved a 60 mm Norinco rifle grenade over the muzzle of his rifle and clicked it down over the launching rings. He had two of them. The old-style Chinese rifle grenades had one strategic weakness. Unlike modern bullet-trap grenades, you couldn't just shoot the grenade off the muzzle with standard ammo. It took a special ballistite cartridge to launch the grenade. The first bullet in Bolan's mag was a launcher round and the rest standard ammo. His first reload was the same way. There was going to be a critical moment when he would have to change magazines to fire his second grenade. His comrades all shared the same tactical problem.

Bolan lay down in his slit trench. Dust sifted onto his chest as he pulled the camouflaged blanket over the hole.

Mrda spoke across the com link. "Dust, in the distance."

"Copy that."

The big American's dirt bathtub began to vibrate and more dust sifted down through the blanket. Bolan felt more than heard the thunder of engines in the distance. Mrda spoke across the link. "They come. I have visual."

Bolan pushed his selector to semiauto. "All units, wait for my signal."

All units came back in the affirmative. "Copy that, Striker."

"Rover 1, Rover 2, start your engines."

"Copy that, Striker."

"Rad, you have eyes on that 23?"

"Negative, Striker." The Serb made a disgusted noise. "Too much dust."

"Range?"

"One thousand meters and closing. They approach at speed in a skirmish line. Following our trail. Eyes on Goose's smoke to the east."

"Copy that, Rad," Bolan stated.

He loosened the pistol in its thigh holster and took a few deep breaths. His team would either achieve total victory in the first few seconds or else it would turn into a slugfest. Bolan could clearly hear the roar of engines.

"Five hundred meters! Four hundred! Two vehicles will pass very close on either side of your position, Striker! Two hundred!"

"Copy that! Ground teams A and B! On my go! Rover 1 and 2! Take fighting positions! Striker is go!" Bolan erupted out of his trench. NASCAR-worthy thunder greeted him. The technicals roared forward rooster-tailing a tsunami wall of red dust in their wake. The range was fifty yards and closing. A primer gray pickup sporting dual-mounted general-purpose machine guns in the back came dead-on. Bolan put the nose of his rifle grenade on the grille of the oncoming pickup and fired.

The rifle slammed against his shoulder as the one-and-a-half-pound grenade thudded through the air.

The front of the pickup disappeared in a blast of smoke and fire. Bolan flicked his selector lever as the pickup stood on its nose and somersaulted. The scream of the man sitting behind the machine guns was lost as he was smeared away. Bolan swung his muzzle onto the next-closest vehicle and burned the rest of his magazine into it on full-auto. He dropped back behind his rocks and stripped out his spent mag. Slapping in a reload, he clicked his second grenade down over his smoking muzzle. Bullets started hitting his position in swarms. Bolan suddenly had the technical swarm's full attention.

"A Team! Now!"

A and B Team both had dug themselves genuine foxholes they could stand in. Ching and Lkhümbengarav threw off their camouflage. Ching fired, and his comrade's grenade launched a heartbeat later. The grenade hit a technical broadside. The truck went sky-high as the grenade detonated the spare shells in a string of spectacular secondary explosions. Lkhümbengarav's munition hit low and detonated beneath his target's chassis. The technical spun out as its guts were ripped out rather than rolling or exploding. Men jumped out of the cab and dived off the back.

"B Team!" Bolan ordered. "Go!"

Pienaar and Tshabalala popped and up and the brothers-in-law fired simultaneously. Pienaar's grenade took his target in the cab. The windows and the roof blew off, and the gunner in the bed screamed as superheated smoke and fire washed over him. Tshabalala's shot slammed against the side of his target and rolled the pickup over like it had been slapped by a fiery hand.

A burst of machine-gun fire chipped rock inches from Bolan's head. The gunner in the back of Lkhümbengarav's first target was still alive, had an angle on Bolan and was looking for payback. The Executioner threw himself flat and brought his weapon to bear. The machine gunner in the back of the technical suddenly flinched forward as though he had been kicked in the back. He jerked twice more and sagged over his weapon.

Mrda and his sniper rifle were in the game.

"Rovers! Go!"

Rover 1 and 2 lurched to the lip of the riverbed.

Ochoa squatted beneath the recoilless antitank gun like he had giant bazooka over his shoulder. He took a second to aim at a Toyota Tacoma with the cab roof sawed off. It carried a Russian .50-caliber rifle and half a squad of Janjaweed in the back. Fire belched from both ends of Ochoa's weapon. The 82 mm artillery round sent man and machine gun cartwheeling through the air in shattered ruins. Ceallach had already slammed open the smoking breech and was loading a fresh shell.

A Russian .50-caliber gun tore into life. Val Onopkov stood in the back of Rover 2. One of the technicals had foolishly slammed on his brakes. The Russian walked his fire up the hood and into the cab. The driver shuddered and flailed and painted the interior red with arterial spray. Onopkov kept walking his fire higher, and the two men in the back manning a mortar tube came apart like straw men. The Russian lowered his aim once more and put a burst through the grille to destroy the engine. The two remaining technicals had made hard turns and were running for their lives.

Bolan lowered his rifle. His rifle grenade had a short range, and he decided to save it. Onopkov's machine gun stitched one of the fleeing vehicles until it slowed to a stop. A and B teams poured fire into the other vehicle from their rifles. A moment later the Russian's weapon joined the fusillade and the last vehicle slowed to a stop, manned only by the dead. The Sudanese plain became eerily silent. Nothing moved except plumes of smoke rising from the wreckage

Bolan removed his rifle grenade and loaded a magazine without a launching cartridge. "Rad, any movement?"

"None visible."

"Right, A and B teams, we sweep the vehicles. Rover 1 and 2 hold position. Haitham, Shartai come forward. Rad, keep an eye on our six."

Haitham and Shartai trotted up as A and B teams climbed out of their foxholes and fell in to form a loose line with Bolan. The air stank of burning gasoline, high explosive and roasting flesh. Five of the nine enemy vehicles were burning. The rest were filled with perforated humans. Tshabalala was grinning. "Aces, Striker! Textbook ambush, 'cept you threw away the textbook!"

Bolan nodded in acknowledgment, then clicked his com link. "We're clear. Lucky, pick up the weapons. Haitham, Shartai, give him a hand. Everyone who shot, top off your magazines. See if a few belts of their fifties survived for Val. We pile and burn everything else. T.C., Russo, check the bodies for anything of interest, then torch the rest of the vehicles." Bolan shot Tshabalala a look. "Yes, you can loot the bodies, but spread the wealth around."

"Aw, Striker, I wasn't even—"

"Sancho," Bolan continued, "grab the siphon. I want to top off our vehicles with their gas and fill our empty cans."

Lkhümbengarav had clambered up into one of the vehicles Onopkov had stitched. He patted the tube of the mortar in the back. "Nice 81 here. Twenty-four rounds of ammo. We want it?"

"We definitely want that. Break it down and put it in the truck when it gets back. Speaking of the Mog, Goose, once we have the area policed up you and T-Lo bring it back."

Bolan's team swiftly went about their jobs. He peered back along their trail. It had gone nearly exactly as he'd hoped. The enemy had been annihilated and his men and machines hadn't taken a scratch. The only problem was that Mnan had operated to expectations. He had sent his lighter vehicles ahead to waylay the caravan. That meant there were still nearly a hundred horsemen and four 23 mm automatic cannons still on their trail; and Bolan wasn't sure whether this action would finally warn Mnan off or put him on a mission from God.

8

Nelsonne was having a bath. Ochoa, Ceallach and several other members of the team kept developing errands that would take them into the vicinity. The woman had rigged two shelter halves to form a shower stall, but Mrda stood guard against unwanted spectators.

Bolan walked up to him. "How's it hanging?"

Mrda started to say something as Bolan walked past him. The soldier rapped on the fender of the Unimog. "You decent?"

"You tell me!"

Bolan came around the corner. A pair of camouflage tarps stretched between the Unimog and Rover 1. They artfully allowed a view of Nelsonne's collarbones up top and calves below. She was bathing out of a bucket. The woman grinned at Bolan and squeezed her hands together. Her soap squirted up into the air in an arc and then fell with a plop in the bucket. *"Mon dieu!"* Nelsonne simpered. "I have dropped the soap!"

Bolan laughed.

The Frenchwoman bent to retrieve it. She winked at Bolan from beneath the edge of the tarp as she reached into the bucket. "You should come in. The water is fine."

"I think Lucky has dibs on the next bath, then Sancho."

"Well, I have always wanted to have a ménage à trois with a reasonable facsimile of Genghis Khan and a…" Nelsonne sought for the word. "Gangbanger?"

Bolan folded his arms across his chest and leaned back against the Unimog while Nelsonne soaped. "So, what is a nice girl like you doing surrounded by men like us in a place like this?"

"The last time I was in the United States I went to the Salinas rodeo in California. I developed an inexhaustible need for cowboy hats and boots. One hundred thousand euros will help put a dent in my desires."

"I don't think you're being completely frank with me."

"I suspect you already know that Frenchwomen like to maintain an aura of mystery, but you must admit you have not been perfectly frank with myself or the rest of the team. I will admit I truly enjoy beating up Sudanese soldiers and killing Janjaweed, except that we might be expecting Sukhois fighters at any time? I know nothing about our mission."

"What do you suspect?"

"Despite brilliant successes against Captain Osmani and Yellow Mnan, this is clearly a rescue mission of some sort, or if not a rescue, an extraction. Willing or not."

"What is French Intelligence's interest?"

"You do not believe my story about needing one hundred thousand euros for hats and boots?"

"I think it's like the Kong brothers getting to kill Janjaweed. It's a glorious perk of the job."

Nelsonne pouted. "Suspicion is your least attractive trait."

"You have great calves."

"Thank you!" Nelsonne bounced up and down on her toes. "I have worked very hard to make them so!"

Bolan took in the woman's gleaming calves and fresh-scrubbed face. He reminded himself that most intelligence agencies kept some drop-dead ringers around. A beautiful woman could take a man off his guard and off his game. They were never just bimbos. They were highly trained intelligence agents who also happened to be smoking-hot. "You're just not going to give me anything, are you?"

"What do you want?"

Bolan deliberately bid low. "Val and Rad, Chechnya and the Congo?"

"Yes, both Onopkov and Mrda served in those conflicts

respectively, and I can see what you are thinking. I do not believe I endanger French national interests if I reveal that both men subsequently served in the French Foreign Legion and rose to the rank of *Caporal de Chef* and *Sergent* respectively."

Bolan knew all too well that the DGSE took the ready-made pool of already highly trained soldiers from all nations that the Foreign Legion provided and trained likely candidates to become field agents. It was very likely that Bolan had an active French Direct Action team on his roster. The question was whether her team and his were on the same mission and wanted the same outcome.

"I could take Rad, Val and Rover 1 and split off, if you would prefer," Nelsonne suggested.

"Nah, I need every swinging dick on this one."

Nelsonne giggled. "And they say Americans have no poetry in their souls." The French agent became serious. "And what will you do for me?"

"Your back?"

She smiled from ear to ear.

YELLOW MNAN TASTED ASHES. From Tripoli to Mogadishu the technical was the sign of a North African warlord's wealth and power. Mnan's fleet, indeed, what he liked to refer to as his armada, lay in twisted, crumpled, smoking ruins. Mnan had carefully built himself up from a penniless albino outcast. He had stolen a horse and slit a sleeping man's throat for a Kalashnikov so he could join a raggedy band of Janjaweed. He had taken over that band by force of will, religious fervor and a murderous hand. He had risen from Janjaweed scum to a tacitly recognized Sudanese militia commander. Mnan sighed as he looked across smoldering ruins and rotting, scavenger-torn flesh.

Mnan knew it could have been worse. He could have been with the flying brigade of technicals he had sent ahead of him to stop the American crusader's convoy while he had come up with the horsemen to close the trap. The fact was he still had nearly a hundred men in the saddle and under arms. He also had his pride and joy. Mnan looked back at his Russian KAMAZ flatbed utility truck and the quad-mounted 23 mm cannons in the back. The gunner gave him a wave. Poti had shot down a Chadian attack plane, a helicopter gunship and destroyed several armored cars. The waste he had laid on Christian and animist farming communities in Darfur with his cannons would best be described as Old Testament worthy. Clay walls and mud huts stood no chance against Poti's cannons, and Mnan's will was Poti's hand.

Mnan ran his eye across the carnage once more. He hated the American. He would stake him out naked upon the earth. He would hold the leash of his best hyena bitch and force her to selectively rip bits off the infidel devil.

Mnan knew what he had to do. He'd produce the 23 mm cannons at a time of his choosing, when he had the Yankee and his mercenary scum exactly where he wanted them. To make that happen he would fight as his ancestors had fought from time out of mind; how North Africans had fought since the time of the English, the French, the Crusaders, the Romans and the Egyptians before them. Like his horse-nomad forebears before him, Mnan would shadow his enemy, probe for weakness, wait for his more heavily armored foe to exhaust himself, and then take his terrible revenge.

Makur stalked forward. "Commander?"

"Brother?"

"The herders behind us, the ones we left money and phones to keep us informed."

"Yes?"

"There is a United Nations convoy behind us."

Given current events Mnan found that very hard to believe, except that the United Nations was infinite in its foolishness. "Oh?"

"Yes, but it is not a normal United Nations convoy."

"And how is it abnormal, my brother?"

"The vehicles are painted white and bear the United Nations emblazon."

"But?" Mnan questioned.

"Every vehicle is armed."

"Armed?"

"Our contacts are surprised." Makur grinned. "They have

never seen the United Nations deploy technicals under UN auspices, much less ones driven by the Chinese."

OCHOA RAN A RAG OVER the recoilless gun. He hadn't gotten his bath. Lkhümbengarav was wrenching under the hood of the Mog. The Mongolian hadn't gotten his bath, either. Everyone noticed Bolan's dust-free and dewy appearance. Everyone noticed Nelsonne was glowing as she clambered into the Unimog's cab. A few winks were exchanged.

"How are we doing, Lucky?" Bolan asked.

Lkhümbengarav stuck his head out. Like everyone else except Bolan and Nelsonne he was covered with dust and sweat. Now his hawk face was smeared with grease and assorted engine filth. He hawked and spit. "It's the dust. I switched out the air filters. She should be fine now. Next stop I'll do a preemptive oil and filter change on the Rovers."

"Thanks, Lucky."

"No problem, GI. Can I have a bath now?"

Bolan looked at his watch, the sun and the rest of the team finishing their rations. "Make it quick."

Pienaar's voice crackled across the radio. The South African was ten klicks back pulling picket duty at the entrance to the low series of hills the convoy was threading "Striker!"

Bolan clicked his com link. "What have you got, Goose?"

"Rotor noise, coming out of the west."

The entire team came to attention. Lkhümbengarav raised his eyebrows at Bolan in question. The big American jerked his head at the Unimog and the mechanic scrambled to deploy one of their two shoulder-launched surface-to-air missiles from the back. Bolan's gaze turned westward. "Can you give me a rotor count, Goose?"

"Sounds like one, Striker, but a big one, and flying low. Sky is clear. He must be flying nap of the earth."

The Sudanese air force had between twenty and thirty Hind-24 helicopter gunships in an operational state at any given moment. Just one of the Soviet-era flying tanks would put an end to the mission and everyone in it. Lkhümbengarav handed off the

HongYing 5 launcher to Ceallach and clambered onto the roof of the Unimog. The Briton handed the weapon back up to him. The Mongolian flicked off the unit's safety and powered up infrared homing in the rocket. "Ready, Striker!"

"Val! Rad! Rover 2!" Onopkov jumped behind the big .50-caliber gun in Rover 2 and racked the bolt on a fresh belt of ammo. Mrda slid behind the wheel. Bolan cut his hand south. "Take position one hundred yards south! Sancho, get Rover 1 the same difference north and set up the .30 in the truck bed! I don't want to lose the whole convoy in one rocket run!"

Rover 1's and Rover 2's rear wheels spit dust as they scrambled to put distance between themselves and the Unimog. Tshabalala jumped into the Mog's cabin and threw open the roof hatch. He racked the .30-caliber gun and pointed his weapon west alongside Lkhümbengarav. Bolan scooped up his rifle and flicked the selector to full-auto. The Hind gunship had been designed to withstand direct hits from automatic cannons. The Mongolian's HongYing 5 was a Chinese knockoff of a not particularly effective Russian shoulder-launched SAM.

"Everyone disperse! Rifle grenades if you got them!" Bolan ordered.

A hit with a rifle grenade would be sheer dumb luck, but the SAM and a series of aerial explosions just might send an inexperienced Sudanese pilot scrambling for home. Bolan clicked his last antiarmor grenade onto his weapon's muzzle. "Goose, you got eyes on?"

"Not yet! But he's right on top of me! He's—" Bolan could hear the rotors through Pienaar's unit. "Eyes on, Striker! It's a Super Frelon! Civilian white-and-blue paint job! No visible markings! They have a door gun! Men and equipment in the back! Men armed and in camo!"

"He see you, Goose?"

"Negative, Striker! I'm in a bit of thornbush! He's heading straight for you!"

Nelsonne called from behind a rock a dozen meters away. "It seems a bit suspicious!"

"Just a bit!"

The Frenchwoman brandished her rifle. "And?"

Bolan clicked his com link. "I want a look at these guys. Wait on my signal."

The news was met with grumbling but everyone copied back. Bolan unscrewed his rifle grenade and replaced it in his fighting vest. He could hear the medium transport's blades slamming the sky. Bolan raised his binoculars as the chopper thundered over the little canyon. The Super Frelon was vaguely whale-shaped. The Executioner stared the pilot straight in the face through his optics. The man was Chinese, as was the copilot. Both crewmen started in alarm at the sight of the heavily armed and spread-out convoy. The door gun ripped into life and began stitching a line of dirt fountains straight for the Unimog.

Bolan clicked his com link. "Hit them!"

Rifles popped and cracked on full-auto and Onopkov's .50 jackhammered into life. Lkhümbengarav's SAM sizzled out of its tube. The pilot violently banked away spewing infrared flares from both sides of the fuselage as if it was the Fourth of July. Shiny objects easily distracted the HongYing 5, and the Mongolian swore as his missile veered hard to go flying after a falling flare. Bolan dropped his binoculars on their strap and brought his rifle to bear. Flame stuttered from his muzzle as he put thirty rounds into the French helicopter in passing. Onopkov swung the big .50 around on its mount and poured fire into the aircraft's aft section. He was rewarded as smoke belched out of the chopper's exhausts and its banking maneuver turned into an ugly half-controlled slide across the sky.

Bolan had already reloaded and was running straight for Rover 1. "Scotty! Lucky! With me!" The big American took the shotgun position and got behind the hood-mounted .30 caliber gun. Ochoa had already taken the gunner's position beneath the recoilless gun. The springs creaked as Ceallach jumped in the back and slammed a shell into the weapon's breech. Lkhümbengarav jumped behind the wheel and put the pedal down. The Mongolian sent the Rover streaking out of the little canyon and precipitously straight up a hillside. The Rover bucked and leaped, and nearly rolled and tipped over backward. Ochoa whooped, Ceallach made a noise that sounded suspiciously like fear and Bolan held on for dear life. Lkhümbengarav was grinning as he gripped the wheel and muttered some kind of Mongolian mantra beneath his breath. He aimed straight for the top. Black smoke was trailing up into the air somewhere behind it.

The vehicle crested the hill without losing any men or matériel.

The chopper had sat down between Bolan's hill and the next. The range was six hundred yards. The Super Frelon was smoking, but her rotors were still turning. Ochoa declinated the tube of the recoilless gun on its mount. "Striker—"

Bolan clapped his hands over his ears. "Hit them!"

Five motorcycles burst out of the chopper's cargo cabin and spit blue smoke as they charged forward. The recoilless heavy machine gun unleashed thunder. Bolan's eardrums tried to meet in the middle of his head as the chopper tipped over with the blast. The rotors snapped off as they struck the ground, and the Frelon tipped back onto its wheels.

The soldier ignored the ringing in his ears and leaned into the hood-mounted PKM. The bikers streaked for a gap in the hills. Bolan walked his tracers into the back of one of the bikers, and the rider popped a wheelie and fell off his bike. The other four went airborne for a moment as they hit a dip and disappeared into the hills. Ceallach opened the smoking breech of the recoilless gun and shoved in a fresh shell. He slammed the breech shut with a clang and slapped Ochoa on the shoulder, but there was nothing left to fire at.

Lkhümbengarav yawned at his ringing ears. "You want to go after them?"

Bolan shook his head. "We'll never catch them. Not in the Rover."

Ochoa slapped the barrel of his recoilless antitank gun. "Four guys on bikes? No refuel? No supplies? Those *vatos* won't get far. We hunt 'em down easy."

"They're not going far, Sancho."

"No?"

"I know you were busy, and good shooting, by the way, but did you notice how they were armed?"

"Uh…no."

Bolan handed Ochoa his binoculars, who took a look at the rider the big American had brought down. He paused as he took in the long, black, scope-sighted rifle lying a few yards from its owner. Ochoa's shoulder sagged. "Aw, shit."

"Those *vatos* are snipers, Sancho, and now they're hunting us."

9

Captain Osmani and Yellow Mnan regarded each other beneath a flag of truce. The two men had never met, but they were aware of each other. Both men were predators who feasted on the bones of the Sudanese civil wars. Their bread and butter was human misery and as the open warfare ran down, competition for that invaluable resource was getting stiffer. Two African-apex predators found themselves on the same hunting grounds. Osmani believed Mnan even uglier than he had been led to believe and his men as raggedy as beggars. Mnan knew Osmani's reputation, but the captain's broken nose and swollen jaw made Mnan wonder about a warlord who let himself get beaten up in front of his men by an unarmed man. Mnan made only a token effort to conceal his speculation. The albino ran his eyes over Osmani and Rao's caravan. Once they had entered the wasteland the Chinese SUVs had sprouted weaponry. "Very pretty," Mnan said. "I had eleven technicals of my own. Then I ran into your American."

Osmani made little attempt to hide his contempt. Rao was eyeing the quad-mounted 23 and the milling horsemen. "How many men do you have under arms?"

Mnan shrugged. "Perhaps four score and ten."

Rao nodded thoughtfully, and it was abundantly clear what he was thinking.

"I saw a helicopter pass over," Mnan commented. "It was flying very low and very fast."

"That was mine," Rao allowed.

"Was?"

"The American destroyed it."

"Yes." Mnan nodded sympathetically. "He is very annoying that way."

"However, I have managed to insert a pair of sniper teams ahead of him."

"Interesting." Mnan ran his eyes over the caravan. "I gather you are about to suggest we pool our resources?"

"The thought had occurred to me."

Captain Osmani put his hands on his hips. "Of course, I am in command."

Mnan looked back and forth between Osmani and Rao and smiled. "Of course you are."

Osmani scowled. Corporal Kiir bristled behind him. Mnan ignored both soldiers and smiled at Rao. "Now, what is this about snipers?"

"SHOW OF HANDS," Bolan said. "Besides Rad, how many snipers do I have?" Ching, Nelsonne and Ceallach raised their hands. "T.C.?"

"I am sniper qualified, though in the three sniper missions on which I was deployed I acted as the spotter."

"Good enough. Russo?"

Nelsonne shrugged. "I trained as a sniper with the DGSE, but I must tell you it was strictly for urban operations and I was never deployed in the role."

"Scotty?"

"I qualified as sharpshooter for my unit, pretty much the same as you Yanks' 'designated marksman.'"

"Rad, you ever deploy?"

Mrda stared at Bolan for several long, measuring moments and lit himself a cigarette. "Sarajevo."

"Sniper alley?"

The Serb blew smoke and considered the glowing tip. "Yes. Twenty confirmed kills."

Bolan measured the man. "Sniper Alley" had become the nickname of Sarajevo's main boulevard during the Bosnian conflict. It connected the industrial district to Old Town and was lined with high-rises. For a small window in time in the 1990s it had been considered the most dangerous place on Earth. Both sides had considered NGO workers, UN peacekeepers and civilians fair game.

"Right, two teams. T.C., you're spotting for me," Bolan said. "Scotty, you're spotting for Rad. Ideally these guys want to put the convoy in a cross fire, shoot a driver or two and pin us down while God knows who else is coming up behind us. If we don't show in the next twenty-four hours, they're going to break position and come creeping in on us and try to disable our vehicles. We don't have the time to waste to lay a countertrap, so we're going to creep them now."

Bolan had only gotten a quick look at the Chinese team. "T.C., what kind of armament are we expecting?"

"The primary sniper-shooter will carry a JS rifle. They are accurate to outside eight hundred meters. The spotters will have semiautomatics with scopes. Either QBU-88s or Dragunovs like Rad's."

Mrda blew three smoke rings and bull's-eyed them with a thin stream of smoke as they expanded. "Were I them, I would expect some kind of attack."

"Me, too, but if the Chinese have been in contact with the guys behind us, they know we're packing light support weapons. They'll be betting we'll try to punch our way out. I don't think they'll be expecting a sniper team, much less two of them. Their motorcycles have left an easy trail."

Ching grimaced. "One they will be watching if they are clever."

"That's why one team will split off wide and shadow the other."

Ceallach scratched his head. "Not to be a total arsehole, squire…"

"You?" Bolan shook his head. "Never."

The Briton snorted. "Right, then. Who's Team 1 and who's Team 2?"

"T.C. and I are Team 1. You and Rad are Team 2. You'll break wide, shadow us and have our six when and if the firefight starts.

If we spot the enemy first, you and Rad will flank them. None of them get back on their bikes to run ahead and try again tomorrow night. Clear?"

Everyone was clear.

"Lucky, how are we on rifle grenades?"

"Low on the antiarmor. We used up about half on the technicals. Still got a crate of frags."

"Issue two frags to the spotters. Issue each team member four hand grenades. Two frags, a concussion and a Willie Pete. Break out night-vision gear. Hand me the green rifle case from the back."

"On it." Lkhümbengarav loped for the small armory in the back of the Unimog. Bolan's sniper teams lined up for gear. Kurtzman had arranged the convoy's weapons locally and most were Chinese. However, Bolan had brought along a personal item or two. The Mongolian handed Bolan his case and the warrior unlimbered his rifle. The M-24 Sniper Weapon System was standard U.S. Army and Marine Corps issue. Bolan's weapon chambered the .338 Lapua Magnum cartridge and sported a 12.2 X magnification Day/Night weapon sight. The big Lapua round was accurate out to 1,500 meters. If they could spot the enemy first, they could stop them from range.

Ochoa sighed happily at the sight of the weapon. "Now we're talking the real shit!"

Bolan checked the battery and the functions on his sight. "Lucky, get Rover 2 reconfigured. Val and Shartai are your team. My people will sync with your GPS and vector you if it comes down to it."

"Copy that, hot rod."

"Goose, you're in charge of the convoy. Don't advance Rover 1 or the Mog unless given the signal or something is coming up behind you."

"Affirmative, Striker."

"Speaking of behind, T-Lo?"

"Yes, Striker?"

"Take some high ground and keep an eye on our six."

"Right!"

The sun was sinking fast behind them. Bolan racked his bolt on a live round and nodded to his team. "Let's go hunting."

EVEN BY NIGHT VISION four motorcycles left a clear trail. Just as clearly one Chinese sniper team had split off. Four sniper teams were doing a slow circling, flanking dance of death. Bolan swept his night-vision-goggled gaze across the flat, broken hills of the Sudan. The question was, which Chinese team had taken fighting point and which was off in the counterpunch position. "T.C.?"

"Yes, Striker?"

"You're Chinese, right?"

"A number of responses come to mind."

"Pair of PRC sniper teams. What do you think?"

Ching calculated. "It is only recently that PRC units, even special forces, have been encouraged to show initiative. By all appearances you took out their commanding officer. It is very likely they will fall back on orders and doctrine. Their best team will take lead, as a matter of seniority, and the second team act as flanker. I wonder why we have done the same?"

"We're the best team, and we took lead because we have a better chance of spotting the enemy first. Rad is experienced, but like Russo, all his instincts were developed in urban fighting. Scotty is a marksman, not a sniper. They put their best forward out of pride."

"You put us forward because you think you and I outclass our opponents."

"Correct."

"Interesting," Ching stated.

"Do me a favor."

"What is that?"

Bolan looked around the ring of hills. His instincts told him they were getting very close to the enemy. "Load a grenade on the end of your rifle."

"Very well."

Bolan clicked his com link. "Scotty, load a rifle grenade."

"Roger that, Striker."

Mrda came back across the line. "You think we are close?"

"What do you think?"

"Yes, I agree," Mrda replied.

"Rad, I want you and Scotty to—"

Ceallach's voice snarled over the com link. "Shit!"

A second later a rifle shot echoed through the low hills. The enemy hadn't gone far. "Scotty!" Bolan hissed. "Sitrep!"

Mrda's Dragunov cracked twice in quick succession. Ceallach groaned across the link. "I'm bloody well shot!" The Briton followed that statement with a stream of arcane cockney epithets.

Bolan swept the hills with his optics. "Rad, you got a position on the shooter? Sitrep on Scotty."

"Time from hit to sound of discharged implies long range. Bullet has passed through left arm. I do not know if bone is broken. Wound slants down. They are above. Using north as twelve, estimate shot came from our nine or ten o'clock."

Bolan scanned through his optics. By Mrda's estimate, the Chinese shooter had put one through Ceallach at slightly over six hundred meters at night.

Ching gazed through his Day/Night laser range-finding binoculars. "I agree with the Serb's estimate. I do not see them, but they are there."

Bolan agreed. Mrda spoke in his ear. "Scotty's bleeding is controlled. He cannot shoot. I am putting his arm in—"

Ceallach's voice came through Mrda's line. The Englishman's accent got thicker by the second. "Fuckin' 'ell ya 'eathen, socialist savage!"

"Scotty is now ineffective," Mrda concluded.

"Oh, you right bloody son—"

Bolan clicked his com link. "Lucky! You have GPS on my position?"

"Copy that, Striker!"

"Advance Rover 1 one klick from my present position!"

"Copy that, Striker! Inbound! ETA five minutes!"

"Copy that," Bolan said. "Rad?"

"Striker?"

"Do something stupid."

Mrda contemplated his orders. "Very well."

His Dragunov suddenly cracked eight times in rapid succession, the muzzle-blasts erupting like little poppy-colored fireworks. The echoes of the thunder bounced around the hills and died. "No response, Striker."

Ching shook his head. "I do not like this. They should have been willing to risk the sacrifice. They are up to something."

Bolan kept scanning Mrda's nine and ten o'clock hilltops. Ching was right. The enemy had put a hole in the Briton. The chance to put a bullet through Mrda was priceless. Even if it came with lethal payback, it meant that Bolan and Ching would have exposed themselves. And that meant putting the hurt on the second team, as well. Instead the Chinese were standing pat. Ching was right.

The Chinese People's Liberation Army was up to something.

"Fuckin' 'ell, Striker!" Ceallach shouted.

Bolan's voice went cold. "Com discipline, Scotty."

"No! No! No, Striker!" Ceallach shouted. "Ten o'clock high!"

Bolan raised his rifle and scanned the night sky through his 12.5 power optics. His lips skinned back from his teeth. Bad guys were falling like rain. "T.C., range."

Ching shook his head. "Two thousand meters. They will fall behind the hills."

Shooting airborne troops as they floated down and watching them go slack in their straps was one of the most sickening of enemy engagements. Part of Bolan was relieved that they were well out of range of his rifle, but that only meant that he would have to shoot them on the ground when they got close enough and were firing back.

"They're Chengdu Military Region Special Forces Unit," Ching muttered. "Falcons."

Bolan had fought the Falcons before. They specialized in target locating, indicating, airborne insertion and sabotage. They were also the Chinese spec op unit that always got the new toys first. That went a long way in explaining the hole in Ceallach. "T.C.?"

"Yes, Striker?"

"What's on their mind?"

"The PRC, like far too many nations, is often lulled into using their special forces as shock troops rather than operators. They will send the airborne forward. We will be forced to fire. The sniper teams will maintain position and take us out. Failing that they will pin us down, and while they do that the Falcons will overwhelm our positions."

Bolan clicked his com link. "Lucky!"

"Yeah!"

"We have enemy airborne, platoon strength and dropping behind Rad's nine and ten. Bring up Rover 1!"

"Range?"

"Half a klick."

"Copy that. Inbound. Will advise when in position."

"Copy that."

Bolan rounded the horn on the link. "T-Lo, link up Rover 2 and the Mog. Goose, start bringing the convoy forward. The Mog hangs back a good klick. Bring up Rover 2. I want Rover 2 to support Rover 1 with the .50-cal if the enemy attempts to flank."

"Clear as crystal, Striker!" Pienaar responded. "Inbound!"

Mrda spoke from his position on the hilltop. "Here they come."

10

Stony Man Farm, Virginia

"Bear!" Bolan called across the link. "You got eyes?"

Kurtzman looked at his screen. The imaging satellite had a good eye on Bolan and his two teams, and the small army massing against them at half a klick and closing. "I have eyes, Striker! But only for the next ten minutes. Next satellite window will be…" The computer expert furrowed his brow at another screen that showed myriad dotted lines arcing around a three-dimensional view of planet Earth from space. The current satellite track had been green and was now turning yellow. In moments it would turn to orange and then go red as it lost sight of Bolan's little corner of the Sudan. The next closest satellite was far too many dots away, and there was nothing even vaguely orange about it much less yellow or green. "ETA two hours, eleven minutes."

"I need you to coordinate a fire mission, Bear, and I need it now or not at all."

Kurtzman spent a lot more time crunching data than in coordinating a fire mission, but the words "now or not at all" meant Aaron Kurtzman would give it the old college try. "Go ahead, Striker."

"You have eyes on me, the enemy and Rover 2?"

"Hold on, Striker. Adjusting view." Kurtzman pulled his view of the world up the slightest fraction and Rover 1 came into view. "I have the complete scene, Striker. Rover 1 is half a klick behind the hill line on your six. He has stopped."

"Send me what the satellite feed shows."

"Copy that, Striker. I can—"

"Send the same feed to Lucky in Rover 2, and then lay a GPS Coordinates Map across the feed. Down to the meter."

"Um…" Kurtzman's fingers flew across his keyboard. "Feed established. You see it on your phone?"

"Copy that, Bear."

"Lucky, do you have satellite feed?"

Lkhümbengarav had one of Bolan's tablets in Rover 1 with him. The Mongolian came back in the affirmative. "Copy that, Bear. Feed established. I have eyes."

Kurtzman nodded as he came to the tricky part. "Overlaying GPS grid… Hold on…hold on…hold on…" Kurtzman hit Return.

Bolan came back immediately. "I have grid."

The Mongolian laughed out loud. "Copy that, Rover 2 has grid!"

Kurtzman allowed himself a small smile of satisfaction. "Window! Eight minutes, thirty-six seconds and counting!"

"Rover 2!" Bolan ordered. "Fire mission!"

"On your mark, Striker!" Lkhümbengarav confirmed.

"You have eyes, Rover 2?"

"Copy that, Striker!"

"Fire at will, Rover 2."

Lkhümbengarav chuckled happily across the link. "You got it, hot rod!" The Mongolian's voice broke out in command mode. "Fire mission! On my coordinates!"

MEN PINWHEELED BROKENLY through the air. Lkhümbengarav's primary mission as a United Nations peacekeeper, and in coordination with the U.S. involvements in Iraq and Afghanistan, had been the training of native contingents with the ocean of Com-Bloc weapons that were available. He knew a lot about antitank weapons. Bolan watched as Chinese Falcons paid the price as they charged across the open terrain between the hills. It was as if Lkhümbengarav was playing some terrible arcade game of Whac-A-Mole, except that the moles weren't mechanical rodents, they were men, and they had no holes to drop down through and no cabinet of safety.

Lkhümbengarav dropped the hammer, and Falcons took wing or slam-danced with high explosive and crumpled. "Running low on bombs, Striker!"

"Keep two in reserve! Bear, any eyes on the sniper teams?"

"No," Kurtzman replied. "Looks like they're waiting to counter snipe on you."

The enemy knew where Mrda and Ceallach were. Bolan decided to play a card. "Lucky! Be ready! I'm going to try to draw fire from one of the enemy sniper teams!"

"Eyes on, Striker! Bomb ready!"

Bolan nodded at his spotter. "T.C.?"

T.C. popped up and ruthlessly cut down the nearest three Falcons. He dropped down and a split second later a bullet whined off the rocks above his head.

Lkhümbengarav shouted across the line. "I have him!"

Bolan had seen the brief flare of the enemy shot on the opposite hillside.

Kurtzman spoke quickly. "Highlighting!"

Bolan looked at the GPS image overlay. The satellite zoomed, and the two suspicious man-shaped lumps appeared where the shot had come from. A small green x overlaid them along with exact GPS coordinates. "Already have it!" Lkhümbengarav called. "Firing!"

Bolan heard the tube noise. Seconds later the green x overlaid a smoking hole. "Pull back the view, Bear." The view rose in altitude. From the godlike vista Bolan saw about eight Falcons scattering wide into the hills. "Rad, Scotty."

Mrda came back. "We are all right. Scotty is stable."

"Can he walk?"

Ceallach bawled out in indignation. "Bloody fu—"

"Rad, get Scotty to the bottom of the hill. Scotty, walk back to Rover 2 if you feel able, or wait for them to come up."

The Briton came back grudgingly. "Copy that— Oh, 'ell. Oh, bloody 'ell."

Bolan grimaced and looked skyward once more.

"They have a bleedin' tank, don't they?"

A huge covered pallet drifted down between the hills suspended by multiple parachutes. The outline of a vehicle with a main gun was fairly obvious even at distance. The Chinese were dropping armor.

"Lucky, how many bombs you have left?"

"Two, Striker."

"Save them. Do not fire without permission."

"Copy that."

"Bear?"

"Vehicle has landed. Be advised it is outside of mortar range. Falcons are stretched out individually in the hills. I have no eyes on the second sniper team."

"Bear, give me eyes on the armor."

The image on Bolan's phone swerved and dropped down onto a vehicle.

The Executioner held out his phone. "T.C., what is that thing?"

"ZLC2000 airborne fighting vehicle. The PLA's latest."

Bolan watched as it began to rumble forward through the defile between the hills. He didn't like the long thin barrel of its cannon. He cared even less for the rail-mounted antitank missile on top of the turret. "What's he got and how do we crack him open?"

"He has a 30 mm cannon and a .30-caliber coax. That's an HJ-73C missile on top. There will be five troopers riding in the back. They have two firing ports to either side and one through the rear hatch."

"Armor?" Bolan inquired.

Ching watched the vehicle on Bolan's phone. "That is the good news. The ZLC2000 was designed to be dropped from a plane without a pallet. The vehicle's armor is quite thin. The frontal arc is rated to stop a Western .50-caliber machine gun. The sides and top to stop .30-caliber and shell splinters."

Technically Bolan's rifle was .30 caliber, but his weapon fired a bullet half again as heavy as a normal NATO rifle round and did it at 3,000 feet per second. Bolan stripped out the magazine of ammo that was designed to kill men and clicked in one loaded with steel-cored armor-piercing incendiary. The problem was, to get the most out of his round's weight and speed he was going to have to let the AFV get close. Close enough so that its cannon and missile armament would be within spitting distance.

Ching was reading Bolan's mind. "Rover 1?"

Rover 1's recoilless antitank gun would blow the Chinese AFV to hell, but like everyone else in the equation it would have to get far too close for comfort to do it, and be blown to pieces in the process.

Ching sighed. "Tell T-Lo to get on one of the motorcycles and bring up the antiarmor rifle grenades. I will try to get in close."

Bolan regarded the Chinese operative. It took a lot of guts to try to sneak up on an armored vehicle that had weapons pointing in every direction. "Let's keep that as Plan B." Bolan clicked his com link. "Sancho."

"Yes, Striker?"

"You got eyes?"

"Copy that. The Bear has Rover 1 patched through."

"Bring up Rover 1," Bolan ordered.

"Oh man, antitank, *Jefe?*" Ochoa grumbled. "You kidding me? In this rig?"

"Chinese airborne fighting vehicle. I'm going to try to hand him to you on a platter. Do not engage unless ordered."

"Copy that."

"Watch out for their infantry," Bolan stated.

"Copy that."

"Bring up some antiarmor rifle grenades. If I am KIA, T.C. will provide you with a diversion. Engage on his go."

"Copy that, Striker. Inbound."

Bolan turned to his spotter. "T.C., if I get greased, you're the man. If you can't get close enough to take the shot on the AFV, throw a Willie Pete in his way. He'll most likely rumble right through it. Have Sancho on the trigger waiting on the other side. He'll only have one shot before Rover 1 gets shredded."

"I understand."

Bolan looked through his scope and saw the AFV rumbling along the defile. "You wouldn't happen to know the layout, would you?"

Ching smiled slyly. "In fact, I have ridden in one. The power pack is in the right front of the hull. The driver's position is on the left. The commander sits slightly elevated directly behind him in tandem. The driver and commander both have their own hatch and periscopes."

"How many men in the turret?"

"Just the one."

That gave Bolan something to work with. "Go."

Ching scrambled down the hill to link up with the Land Rovers.

Mrda passed him as he made his way up the hill. The Serb flopped down beside Bolan breathlessly. "Scotty is in decent condition and walking back. Rover 2 will pick him up. I will spot for you. The AFV will have men in back. You may need backup."

Bolan lay down behind his rifle. "Glad for the company."

The AFV ground forward into view. Bolan heard the telltale whine of advancing treads and the rumble of diesel. The fighting turret swiveled slowly back and forth, observing the hills around it. The vehicle was buttoned up. Bolan scanned for the weak points. Behind the missile-launch rail and slightly to the left squatted a suspicious-looking cylinder about the size of a five-gallon bucket. The suspicious, inverted, bucket-looking projection sported a dark glass panel about the size of a tablet personal computer. It wasn't the way the U.S. armored corps did it, but Bolan had a feeling that the projection was the turret gunner's observation station. "Range me."

"Two hundred meters."

Bolan put his crosshairs on the armor-glass observation port and fired. He was rewarded by a textbook bullet hole through the little windshield.

"Nice shot," Mrda declared.

For a small, moving target at night, it wasn't bad. Bolan flicked his bolt. The turret of the AFV spun and the barrel of the 30 mm cannon swept the hill like a divining rod looking for water. Bolan put his sights on the exposed HongJian 73 antitank missile sitting on its launch rail. The squat little missile was about three feet long and bore a pleasing resemblance to a 1950s B-movie rocket ship. It was a misnomer that shooting high explosive sent it sky-high. Modern HE was extremely shock resistant and required an electrical, chemical or high-heat trigger to set it off. The HongJian's solid propellant rocket motor, on the other hand, was distinctly susceptible to armor-piercing incendiary rifle rounds. Rocket fuel was contrary that way.

Bolan put his crosshairs between two of the missile's control fins and fired.

The missile shuddered on its launch rail as the bullet struck. A black bullet hole appeared in the rocket's rear hull and smoke oozed out of it. The 30 mm cannon swung toward their position accusingly. Mrda's normally low rumble rose slightly. "He has seen our muzzle-flash!"

Bolan put his sights back on the turret's observation port.

The rocket motor blew up in a beautiful orange pulse of fire. That was enough to coerce the missile's warhead into detonating. The white-hot plasma pulse of the shaped charge sheeted across the AFV's top deck. Mrda sighed. "You are wonderful."

"Thank you," Bolan said. "I've worked very hard to become wonderful."

The Executioner and Mrda went flat and slid down to put the hill between themselves and the target as the 30 mm cannon slammed into life in blind retribution. Geysers of rock and soil erupted into the air above them.

"Second position!" Bolan ordered. Mrda followed as the big American ran thirty yards along the hill line. Bolan clambered back to the top and peered over the rocks. Mrda ran his night-vision binoculars over the AFV. Black smoke rose off the turret and the top deck.

"I believe the turret observation station is still functional," the Serb stated.

Bolan put his crosshairs on the bullet-punched observation glass and fired.

The port screen collapsed and sparks shot as the night-vision camera behind it shattered. Bolan and Mrda went flat again as the coax gun opened up and drew a line of bullets across the hilltop. The usually surly Serb gave Bolan a grin. "With permission?"

"Be my guest."

Mrda popped up and dropped to one knee. His Dragunov cracked, and the spotlight on top of the turret shattered. His body turned with the same mechanical efficiency of the AFV turret below, and he shot out both of the vehicle's headlights. The triple smoke dischargers on both sides of the turret pop-pop-popped! Six smoke grenades detonated in the defile between the hills, and the AFV disappeared in the fog of war.

"We have him," Mrda declared.

"He'll be deploying his men." Bolan clicked his com link. "Sancho! Bring it up quick! Enemy has deployed a smoke screen! Be advised he is probably deploying five troopers from the back! Possible support weapon!"

"Copy that!"

Kurtzman came on the line. "Striker! Be advised, remaining Falcons are moving forward to link up with the AFV! Location of second sniper team still unknown!"

Between them and the troopers in the back, the enemy still had a squad. "Copy that!" Bolan flicked his bolt and put a round where he knew the AFV should be. He was rewarded by the spark and whine of a ricochet. Mrda put five quick rounds in the same area to keep the AFV's attention on them. The coax gun opened up again and the obscuring smoke lit up with stuttering yellow flashes.

"Striker!" Ochoa called. "In position!"

Bolan glanced at his screen. The defile took a nice bend and Rover 1 could pop out from behind and then pop back, assuming Rover 1 survived the initial exchange. "Wait for it, Rover 1. On my signal!"

"Holding position, Striker!"

"AFV is moving," Kurtzman announced. "Infantry behind, moving from cover to cover!"

Bolan was pretty sure they intended to punch out of the defile and move on to take on the convoy directly while their remaining sniper team played games with Bolan. The Executioner watched as the AFV left its obscuring smoke cloud behind. It wasn't a bad plan. It was just that Bolan had a better one. Ching spoke quietly across the link. "AFV is within range. I have the shot."

"Hold that thought…" The AFV was just about to pass beneath Bolan and Mrda's position. "Rad."

The Serb popped up and fired his 10-round magazine dry as fast as he could pull the trigger. The turret swung toward their position. Rifles cracked in the defile as the Falcons took aim. "Rover 1! Go! Go! Go!"

The AFV unleashed a storm of 30 mm rounds at the hilltop. Rover 1 pulled around the bend and screeched to a halt. Ochoa crouched beneath the recoilless antitank gun. Nelsonne was driving, and Onopkov was behind a light machine gun. Either the AFV's driver or commander saw the danger. The turret spun to bring its cannon to bear on Rover 1. Ochoa took a stomach-dropping extra second to align his sights. The AFV turret came into line. Sancho fired. The AFV's turret disappeared for a split second in the flash and smoke and then erupted like a volcano. A barrage of 30 mm cannon shells cooked off like giant firecrackers and the spare antitank missiles went up in great slams that shuddered the hull. Bolan ignored the fireworks. "T.C., you got eyes on the infantry?"

"They are in a pairs, holding position. One fire team is in range."

Bolan slid a magazine of antipersonnel ammunition into his rifle. "Hit them."

Ching's weapon thumped. The detonation of the rifle grenade seemed anticlimactic after the death of the AFV, but it elicited screams from the men it hit. The other fire teams poured fire into Ching's position in the rocks below. Bolan took out a Falcon, while Mrda took three more in rapid fire. The enemy ceased fire and hugged rock against the plunging sniper fire from below.

"T.C., you all right?"

"I am fine."

"Call on them to surrender."

Ching spent a moment contemplating this. "Very well…" He shouted out in Mandarin.

Angry shouts met the suggestion.

"Tell them to throw down their weapons and come forward of the AFV. They won't be harmed. If they don't, I'll use the recoilless to blast them out of their positions." Bolan decided to try a lie. "Tell them we have their second sniper team pinpointed. If they don't surrender, I'll bring up my mortar and annihilate them, as well."

This news was met with silent but palpable consternation. The Falcons were some of China's best. In their public operational history they had never lost, much less surrendered, to anyone.

Kurtzman burst onto the link. "Striker! Second sniper team has broken cover. They have split up and are moving eastward at a dead run!"

"Keep an eye on them."

"Striker, be advised I will lose sat window in sixty seconds."

"Copy that." Bolan knew where the sniper team was going. They were heading for their motorcycles, and they were going to set up shop again somewhere down the road. That would have to be dealt with later. Bolan kept his attention on the Falcons in the defile below. "T.C., tell them this is their last chance. If they don't surrender now, we're coming through and we aren't taking prisoners."

Ching shouted once more.

Ochoa spoke from his post behind the recoilless gun. "I have beehive loaded, Striker."

"Copy that. If one of them makes a false move, eliminate all."

A rifle spun through the air and clattered into the defile. Three more followed it. The Falcons came out of cover, arms raised in surrender and shoulders hunched against the expected bullet. Bolan rose. "Rad, hold position. We may have missed one. I want eyes from the heights."

"I understand."

Bolan clicked his com link. "Goose, bring the Mog forward. Lucky, bring up Rover 2."

He shouted down to Ching. "Tell them to get on their knees!"

11

"You are going to let them live?" Nelsonne was slightly incredulous. Most of the team seemed against the idea. The four prisoners knelt miserably in the dust with forlorn looks on their faces as the sun rose. Bolan had allowed them some water and a disgusting meal of gooey rice and reconstituted mystery meat out of their ration packs while the team had gone over the battlefield. There had been little of worth to strip from the burned-out AFV. They had gathered the Falcon's fallen weapons and gear. Bolan was interested to note they were using M-16 A-4 clones. He was much more interested in the support weapons that had been left behind and the hand grenades. Lkhümbengarav had gathered them, inspected them and loaded those still functional into the Mog.

Bolan regarded his captives. They wore no insignia. "T.C.?"

"They are Falcons, on a black operation in the Sudan. Nearly all Falcons speak English. If this team specialized in North Africa, some of them will speak Arabic or French, as well." One of the prisoner's eyes went wide with alarm at this declaration. "For example, this one understands English."

The prisoner spit on Ching and snarled something. Ching sighed and started to turn away. He blurred back around and literally slapped the teeth out of the prisoner's mouth.

"T.C...."

The prisoner collapsed to the dust. Ochoa whooped from the bed of Rover 1. "Whoa, snap! Bitch-slap on the *Hal-con, maricon!*"

"Sancho, shut it. T.C.?"

"He implied that I was a traitor."

Bolan raised a quizzical eyebrow. "To the Republic of China?"

Ching smiled. "No."

"You think they'll talk?"

"I do not know." Ching suddenly cracked his knuckles. "You could try asking them nicely, and then I can try asking not so nicely."

One of the prisoners turned and looked Bolan in the eye. "You guaranteed my men would not be mistreated."

"What's your rank?" Bolan asked.

The Falcon regarded the Executioner frostily. "Your nearest equivalent would be staff sergeant."

"Well, Staff Sergeant," Bolan said with a shrug, "you're free to go."

The staff sergeant blinked.

Onopkov loomed over Bolan. "That is it? You let them go?"

Bolan ignored him. "Lucky, let each have two canteens back and their packs with rations and shelter halves."

Lkhümbengarav looked close to open revolt. Bolan didn't blink. "That's an order."

He was fairly certain this was the first time he had been sworn at in Mongolian, but the men went to the pile of Chinese supplies and broke out rations.

Ching shook his head. "You are making a terrible mistake," he said bitterly.

"It's mine to make," Bolan replied.

Ceallach looked back and forth between the prisoners and Bolan. The Brit's left arm was in a slightly bloody sling. He had confiscated the staff sergeant's Type 80 machine pistol. The weapon hung loose in his hand. "Striker?"

"Scotty?"

"Not that I'm questioning orders."

"Glad to hear it."

Ceallach waved the machine pistol at the prisoners. "But they're elite troops."

"And?"

"And you let them go? We're going to have to bloody fight them all over again, aren't we?"

"That could happen," Bolan said. "But a deal's a deal."

Onopkov drew his pistol. "You are American. I understand. Go for walk. I do it."

"Stand down, Val."

The Russian's normally cold demeanor moved toward an icy sort of anger. Bolan's hand rested loosely on the butt of his Beretta.

"I said stand down." Bolan noted with a small amount of satisfaction that Ochoa had silently taken up his rifle and was pointing it at the Russian's head. Onopkov holstered his pistol and shook his head without looking back. "And do not think I do not know, little man."

Ochoa shrugged. "Val's got, like, ESP or something."

The Falcons shrugged into their packs. The staff sergeant stared at Bolan expressionlessly for a moment, then turned without a word and began marching westward. His men fell into line behind them. The stiff way they walked said they were still expecting the bullet in the back. Bolan watched as they disappeared behind a bend in the hills.

Bolan turned to the little Mongolian. "Lucky, do you still have the tablet I gave you?"

"Of course." The merc reached into the tactical pack he was wearing. "Right here."

"Hit the GPS function."

"Why should—" Lkhümbengarav's smile shone like the sun. "Oh, you are one foxy GI!" He tapped an icon and then another. The team suddenly realized the plan and gathered around.

Bolan nodded. "Tell me we have four signals."

"Hell, yes, hot rod!"

Onopkov looked at Bolan with renewed respect. "You placed tracer."

"I placed four tracers, Val," Bolan said. "Their packs are double-bottomed. Russo and I put radio-frequency IDs along the pack-strap anchor points. Two of the packs are wired for sound.

"The wires are good for about forty-eight hours," he continued. "But they won't go active until my people beam down the right radio signal via satellite. T.C., when I do that, I need you and Lucky switching shifts to monitor 24/7."

Both men nodded.

"The enemy still has a sniper team ahead of us on motorcycles. I'm having my people do a grid-by-grid search for them, but as you know our satellite coverage is spotty. T-Lo, I want you to go ahead and find their tracks. That will at least give my people a starting point."

"Right." Tshabalala slung his rifle and threw a leg over his bike.

"Lucky, reconfigure Rover 2 for the gun-jeep role and stow the mortar. Val, give him a hand. Sancho?"

"Striker?"

Bolan stared eastward toward his objective and where the snipers would be waiting. "Breakfast detail, and get some coffee going."

"IT'S LIKE THE BLOODY Outback," Ceallach grumbled. He watched from the shotgun position in the Mog while Bolan drove. It was currently 104 degrees Fahrenheit. Team members were swiftly becoming ready to kill for cab time in the air-conditioned Unimog. Ceallach was working his wounded arm for every extra second. "Except worse."

Bolan had to agree. The Sudan was huge. It was unfortunately placed below the magnificence of the Sahara but well above the fertile belt of sub-Saharan and Equatorial Africa. What the Sudan was, was almost endless, arid scrub; and Ceallach was right, there were no kangaroos bounding across the plain or truck stops manned by friendly Aussies handing out lagers in oil-can-size containers to relieve the burning, sere monotony. Bolan had been to more places on Earth than most people, and despite the usually heinous circumstances that brought him to the most dangerous corners of the globe, he could usually find something to admire about most localities.

The Sudan always tested that resolve.

"So, Striker..."

Bolan refrained from sighing. "Yeah, Scotty?"

"Listen, pay is good, and I don't mind getting shot now and again, then, do I?"

"You were actually pretty cool about the whole thing," Bolan admitted.

"But bloody hell, Striker. The bleeding great People's Republic of China?"

"Would it make you feel any better if I told you I wasn't expecting their involvement?" Bolan asked.

"Oh, well." Ceallach made a noise. "That's a comfort."

Bolan cracked himself a bottle of water and waited for it.

"Striker?"

"Scotty."

"Bloody hell, then."

The truth was going to come out sooner or later, and Ochoa, despite his checkered past, and Ceallach were the two men he trusted most on the team. "What do you know about smallpox?"

"Had it as a tot."

"No, Scotty—" Bolan restrained himself from rolling his eyes "—you had chicken pox."

"Right, chicken pox. I got all spotty, then."

"Smallpox is the same except you go all spotty and then die."

Ceallach's brows bunched. "Been eradicated, hasn't it?"

"That's true, except that a few countries keep some stockpiles of the virus. The U.S. is one, Russia is another."

"And the Chinese?"

"It's rumored."

"And the bloody Black Plague is here? In the Sudan? And we're driving toward it, then?"

"The Black Death was bubonic plague."

"Oh, well, sorry, Striker. We're driving toward smallpox. Don't know if I had my injections for that."

"Given your age you probably did."

"Oh, well, bloody fucking—"

"But the point is, it's been eradicated. There's a whole generation of humans who haven't been inoculated against it. If you want to build a biological weapon, smallpox is your dream virus.

Ninety-plus percent lethal and easily communicable. Since it's been eradicated, the vaccine is in extremely short supply. For an afflicted population the only treatment is supportive. You survive it or you don't."

"Yeah, we were educated about biologicals a bit in the service. But it's bloody suicide, isn't it? How do you keep it out of your population? No place on the bloody planet is more than twenty-four hours from any other," Ceallach pointed out.

"That's right, but what if you could weaponize it? What if you could tailor it?"

Ceallach grew distinctly unhappy. "We had a black bloke in my squad, back in the day. He swore the U.S. government invented AIDS to kill his people."

"From everything I know, AIDS came from Africa, Scotty. But imagine a virus that only attacked those with certain genetic markers. Like your squad mate said, one that only killed people with a preponderance of African gene markers. Or one that killed people with a preponderance of Japanese gene markers and not Chinese. Or one that you could introduce into London and it only killed East Enders like you."

"So…someone in the Sudan has weaponized it?"

"The one person on Earth at the moment who knows how to, is."

Ceallach nodded. "Like Russo said, an extraction, willing or not."

"That's pretty much it."

"Right, then, who is this bloke?" Ceallach probed.

"It's a bird."

"Pretty bird, then?"

"Yeah, she's easy on the eyes," Bolan said.

The Briton grinned. "Bob's your uncle!"

"Yeah, well, while you're bobbing and uncling, I have a favor to ask."

"Name it, Striker."

"Right now I trust you and Sancho implicitly."

"'Preciate that, Striker."

"So you have a busted wing," Bolan stated.

Ceallach tapped the machine pistol at his side. "Right, baby-sitting detail. Got it. Guard the package."

"Yeah, and one other thing."

"And what's that, then?"

"If I go down, and the mission goes FUBAR?"

He gave Bolan a leery look. "Right…?"

"Terminate the package."

Ceallach bowed his head and spent long moments contemplating the tips of his boots in the Mog's footwell. "All right."

"One other thing?"

"Aw, hell…"

"If I go down, and Russo and her team get hinky, kill them, too. I'm going to put Sancho in the know with the same orders."

Ceallach sighed heavily and raised his head. "Right, then."

"That's messed up." Ochoa wasn't happy.

Bolan passed the canteen of powdered sports drink they were sharing as they did maintenance on Rover 1. "Sancho?"

Ochoa's tattooed Adam's apple bobbed as he took three long pulls and passed it back. "Yeah?"

"You can say no. You're still my recoilless man. You're still one of two people I implicitly trust on this one. It's an ugly job and I only want volunteers."

"Listen, *Jefe*. This Señorita of the Apocalypse we're looking for? I'd cap her in a second. But Russo? We've fought together. She's pulled her weight. She's part of the team."

"I know," Bolan replied.

"Dude, I've had thoughts about that woman."

"I know, it's been noted. You need to stop that. I can't have my support-weapon man degrading his eyesight."

Ochoa raised his hands to heaven. "You're killing me."

Bolan's phone vibrated. "Glad we had this talk, Sancho." Bolan walked a little ways away while Ochoa went back to wrenching. "Bear, tell me we have a location."

"We have a very strong candidate, though it took one hell of a grid search to find it. The Sudan is huge."

Bolan glanced around the broken horizon. "Yeah, it is."

"It's a large encampment and, given the availability of water, it is most likely at least semipermanent. Given her pattern of moving from camp to camp, it's the most likely choice, and given the size, she's likely to stay for a while. I'm sending you the coordinates and the satellite images now."

Bolan considered his fuel. "How far?"

"At your current pace? I'd say between 48 to 72 hours, but where you're going the closest thing to a road is a herding route. It's going to be some rough terrain. I can't advise traveling at night unless it's an emergency."

The whole situation was an emergency, but a snapped axle would leave Bolan at the mercy of his enemies. "I'm getting a real strong feeling that Russo and the DGSE know the nature of the mission."

Kurtzman was quiet for a moment. "Yeah, me, too."

"Any way you can connect the French in all this?"

"One link, but it's tenuous, and we're having problems getting any verification."

"What's that?" Bolan asked.

"One of the target's assistants is Canadian."

"Let me guess. Quebec."

"That's right."

French Intelligence had a presence in Canada. Mostly they engaged in industrial espionage against North America, but Bolan knew from firsthand experience they kept some genuine field agents and reaction teams on hand, and Quebec was their HQ. "Good to know."

"So what are you going to do now?" Kurtzman asked.

"We've got an advantage in that we don't know where we're going. Neither does the enemy, so they're following us. The Chinese must have eyes on with satellites, but if my satellite windows have gaps theirs must be a lot worse. I want to make a real serious attempt to break contact with these assholes once and for all."

"I suppose we could help you arrange something," Kurtzman offered.

"But before we do that I need a grid-by-grid map of the territory a hundred klicks ahead and fifty klicks wide."

"The snipers."

"If I'm going to turn and fight," Bolan said, "I can't have them on my six. The enemy doesn't know where we're going, so the snipers ahead of us won't have gone far."

"I'll have your grid-by-grid cordon within the hour."

"Thanks, Bear."

"Striker, good hunting."

"Thanks."

12

Bolan and Mrda hunted. The Sudanese scrub wasn't flat. The landscape rolled and dipped. It rarely rained. When it did, it came in torrents and flood-carved ravines scored the landscape like raddled, unhealed scars. Sand-scoured rock formations thrust forth from the scrub, and inexplicable piles of boulders littered the landscape. It wasn't quite a sniper's paradise, but it was bad enough. The shot could come from anywhere. With Kurtzman's help they had found the spot where the Chinese sniper team had remounted its bikes. Their mission hadn't changed. The job would be to slow the convoy, or better yet, pin it down, ideally disabling one or more vehicles and disabling a team member or two in the process. It was a simple mission, but it also gave clues to their location. They were on off-road motorcycles and the convoy was in trucks. The Chinese would position themselves where they knew the convoy would have to pass, and would stay fairly close to prevent the convoy having multiple options.

Bolan had taken the satellite mapping that Kurtzman had sent him and picked the most likely sites. The Chinese had tried to throw them off by taking their bikes across an expanse of slick rock, but the tires had scuffed the surface, leaving an open trail. Bolan skirted the shingled expanse of rock and moved into the gullies and hills. The land was slowly and steadily rising.

Mrda glanced back and pointed. "From here the enemy had good shot."

"I know." Bolan pointed ahead. "There."

The Serb's brows bunched mightily and he made some sort

of Slavic noise that was half derisive and half concerned. Bolan shared Mrda's concern. The enemy position was a rock formation erupting out of the side of a low hill, looking vaguely like a castle, right down to three almost symmetrical crevices in the rocks like firing slits. The position was frontally impregnable. It was also the most incredibly obvious strong point for two klicks.

"Range me."

"Three hundred and fifty meters," Mrda stated. He turned back and ranged the likely path the convoy would take through the hills. "Seven hundred fifty." The Serb scowled from behind his binoculars as he looked at the strong point again. "It is a stupid hide."

The position would allow both sniper team members to shoot into the convoy when it passed, and at well under their weapons' effective ranges. It would also leave them invulnerable even to Ochoa's return fire with the recoilless rifle. The problem was they might as well have put up a sign that read Chinese Sniper Ambush 750 Meters To Your Right. "They're not waiting for the convoy. They know they're being hunted. They're waiting for us."

"Even more stupid," Mrda muttered. "And I do not believe these Chinese are stupid."

"No," Bolan agreed. "They're up to something."

"What could they be up to? We have their number. Two men on motorcycles with rifles. Perhaps a few hand grenades." Mrda glowered at the rock formation. "I say we flank them."

"They'll be expecting that."

Mrda put a cigarette in his mouth but didn't light it. "You fear a booby trap?"

"We took a few mines off the Falcons." Bolan slid out his phone. "Bear, you got eyes?"

"Currently two klicks ahead of your position, sweeping grid by grid."

Bolan punched the satellite app. "Bear, come back to my position." The Sudan slid beneath the watchful eye of the NSA satellite and Bolan found himself looking at himself and Mrda. He brushed his fingers together to raise the image and tapped the offending rock formation. "You see anything?"

Bolan waited while Kurtzman did his own adjustments on his end. "No, Striker. No movement. Nothing visible."

The Serbian sniper took the cigarette out his mouth, stared at it and put it back. "You wish me to volunteer for what you are thinking?"

Bolan raised a bemused eyebrow. "What am I thinking?"

"I will pop up and put a round through each crevice. You will wait for return fire. Whether it comes from the strong point or elsewhere."

Bolan smiled. "The thought had crossed my mind."

Mrda put his binoculars back in their case and took up his rifle. "I am ready."

"You get that, Bear?"

Kurtzman sighed over the link. "I heard."

Bolan shouldered his rifle and nodded to Mrda. "Go!"

Mrda popped up. His Dragunov cracked three times in rapid succession and he dropped back down. Fire pulsed in two of the crevices and sent chips of stone spattering over Mrda's head. Bolan touched off a shot through the center crevice hoping his steel-cored bullet might get a lucky ricochet.

"I have firing signatures," Kurtzman reported.

"No shit," the Serb muttered.

"But no visible movement," Kurtzman continued. "They're dug in or have covered the top of their position."

"They are there! Both of them!" Mrda was disgusted. "The idiots have given themselves away!"

"No." Bolan shook his head. "We did."

"Striker, I have motion! Two hostiles breaking cover! They're doing…something!"

Bolan snapped his gaze skyward at the sound of a strange, rattling hiss.

"Fuck's sake!" Mrda snarled. "What the hell?"

A small, smoking, dark green object wobbled through the air toward them in a looping arc. The object's flashlight-size rocket motor fell away as a second object hissed up into the air. "Rocket-assisted hand grenade!" Bolan snarled. "Take cover!"

The Executioner grimaced. He'd been foxed. The Chinese

Type 79 rocket-assisted grenade was a gimmick, and one that most armies had rejected and something even Bolan himself had never expected. It was a stick grenade that happened to have a rocket motor in the stick. Issued to the average soldier, aim and trajectory was a Kentucky-windage affair at best.

Then again these men were Falcons, and there was every chance they had practiced with their Type 79 grenades like NFL quarterbacks zinging footballs through swinging tires during spring training. Bolan clicked his com link. "Goose! We're taking fire! Be advised enemy has grenades that can hit the convoy at four hundred meters!"

"Copy that, Striker! Holding position! Do you want Lucky to bring up the mortar?"

"Goose! Hold that thought!" Bolan hugged rock. The first grenade thudded into the baked mud of the gully five yards ahead and detonated with an incredibly loud pop! Shrapnel shrieked off the rocks. The second grenade fell behind them, and Bolan dived over his cover. Mrda followed suit as the second grenade whip-cracked. Serbian curses filled the ravine as the echoes of the detonation died. "Rad! Are you—" Bolan snarled as the sound of two more superduty bottle rockets hissed into the blue. "Incoming!"

The third grenade landed next to the second and both Bolan and Mrda were shielded from the blast. The fourth landed wide on the lip of the ravine and sent a fountain of dirt skyward. Bolan yawned to clear the ringing in his ears. "Rad!"

"Motherfucker!" Rad replied, Bolan kneed and elbowed his way over to the Serb. The sniper was gingerly propping himself up on one elbow and hip. His right hand clamped his right buttock. Blood oozed from between his fingers, staining through his pant leg down the hamstring.

"Goose," Bolan said over his com link. "Rad is hit."

"Copy that. Advise."

"They're hoping you bring up the convoy so they can take their shots. If I don't request the convoy within the hour, you'll contact Bear and he will advise."

"Copy that, Striker. Holding position."

Ching spoke on the link. "Striker, request permission to come forward and assist."

"Negative, T.C. They're coming for Rad and me hard and quick. I either win in the next twenty minutes or you'll be walking into the cross fire alone. If I go down, you're the team's last sharpshooter. Pick a fight with them later with Bear's help."

"Copy that, Striker."

Bolan clicked off and sighed at the Serb. "Didn't I tell you to watch your ass?"

The Serb grimaced as he clutched his bleeding buttock. "You are not as funny as you think you are."

"Assume the position."

"Bastard…"

Bolan ripped open a field dressing. Mrda's starboard butt cheek was full of fragments, but none seemed to have gone too deep. The back of his leg was mostly scored rather than mulched. The Serb's posterior looked like he'd sat on a carton of lightbulbs. Bolan pressed a dressing against the wound and taped it in place.

"Listen, they're coming. The opportunity to kill two of us is too good to give up. They also know we have a mortar we can bring up, so they want to do this fast. They have our position, but they know we're better than they are. They don't want a sniper fight. They gambled on drawing us in and surprising us with the bottle rocket routine and they got half-lucky. I'm betting they're out of rocket grenades, but I'm also betting they have a few hand grenades left."

"They will creep in to finish us."

"That's right."

"What is the plan?" Mrda asked.

"We finish them."

The Serb nodded. "I like this plan."

"You think you can move?"

"I can do whatever is required."

"Good." Bolan took up his rifle. "Bear, where are they?"

"Pincer movement. Approximately two hundred yards and closing."

Bolan secured his phone to his left forearm with a Velcro

strip and examined the image. The enemy had picked its killing ground well. Endless years of flash floods had curved around the rock formation and given the two Chinese snipers nearly parallel courses to Bolan and Mrda's position. The Serb groaned as Bolan threw him into a fireman's carry and slogged through the shattering mud crusts to put a bend in the gully between him and his pursuers.

"Striker!" Kurtzman warned. "You better look at this!"

Bolan kept trudging as he looked at his phone. Kurtzman had a black-and-white dual screen on the Chinese. One was fiddling with something the size of a police flashlight. The other was crouching and appeared to be looking at something the size of a tablet. Bolan stopped. The Falcon looking at his tablet suddenly hunched a little closer to his screen.

"One hundred meters and closing, Striker!"

Bolan stared straight up into the heavens and waved.

The Falcon jerked.

"Bear! They have eyes on!"

"Copy that, Striker!"

The second Falcon hurled his grenade. The munition sizzled into the sky. At that range he had to heave it at a high trajectory. Bolan slid Mrda off his shoulders. "Down!"

The Serb stifled a scream as he sat hard.

Bolan dropped his rifle in Mrda's lap and slapped leather for his Beretta machine pistol. He flicked the selector with his thumb to 3-round-burst mode and waited several seconds for the tumbling grenade to come within range. When the rocket motor fell away Bolan began touching off 3-round bursts as if he was shooting skeet.

"Maniac!" Mrda screamed.

Bolan touched off a second and a third burst as the grenade plummeted toward their position. The big American suppressed a self-congratulatory smile as the grenade sparked and skipped wildly off course. He slapped in a fresh magazine. "Rad, the grenadier has no shot for another fifty meters! Cover me!"

The Executioner scrambled over the lip of the gully and charged. He stabbed out the Beretta and kept one eye on his front sight and one eye on the phone strapped to his forearm. The Falcon was trying to manage his tablet and unsling his rifle. Bolan bounded over the rocks, taking a moment to pull a fragmentation grenade from his vest and pull the pin.

Kurtzman's voice rose. "He's popping up—"

Bolan took his eye off the screen and focused his front sight on the lip of the Falcon's ravine. A long barrel slid upward and slammed down. Bolan touched off a burst and sand flew. He touched off a second and a third.

The Falcon's rifle spoke, and Bolan heard the supersonic crack as the round passed. Mrda's rifle began slamming out rounds in slow precise fire. Bolan touched off two more bursts and hurled his grenade. He dropped flat as a rifle bullet plucked at his cargo pants. The grenade detonated and the Falcon screamed.

Bolan slapped in a fresh magazine and clicked his com link. "T.C., use one of the commandeered Falcon radios. Tell this guy to surrender. He knows we let his buddies live. He knows we have him on satellite. Tell him to surrender or I'll bring up the convoy and mortar him to hell like I did his assault platoon."

"Copy that, Striker." Bolan heard Ching speak Mandarin across the Falcon tactical link. The sniper sounded close to tears. Ching's voice was only slightly smug. "He surrenders."

"Goose, bring up the convoy." Bolan rose and moved to the ravine. The Falcon sniper lay with one hand on his throat and one on his thigh. He was torn by shrapnel, and had bled out through the carotid and the femoral artery. Bolan strode over to the remaining Falcon's position. He was still clutching his rifle. "T.C., tell him to lose the rifle and assume the position."

Ching roared in Mandarin. The Falcon sniper suddenly cast away his weapon. He dropped to his knees and put his hands behind his head. Bolan leaped from the top of the gully and landed behind the sniper. He put a boot between his shoulder blades, knocked him flat then swiftly stripped the Falcon of his weapons and hog-tied him.

Mrda called from where the gully branched. "Striker!"

"Clear!"

The Serb tottered across the crust. Bolan nodded at the unlit cigarette that seemed to be glued to the man's lip. "Smoke 'em if you got 'em." The Serb looked at Bolan helplessly as he tried to perch himself on rock with just his left buttock. With vast effort he positioned himself and lit his cigarette. Bolan sighed sympathetically and clicked his com link again. "Russo, prep for surgery."

13

Mrda glared into some terrible middle distance. The Serb lay draped over the hood of Rover 1 in about as undignified a position as a soldier could assume. A sleeping bag beneath his hips elevated his wounded posterior to Nelsonne's ministrations. Facial tics pulsed across Mrda's face as the French agent tweezed shrapnel out of his posterior without the benefit of anesthetic. The audience was remarkably bereft of sympathy.

"She's got him over a barrel then, doesn't she?" Ceallach remarked.

Ching folded his arms across his chest and shook his head. "I've never seen anything like it."

"Oh, I've seen this in lockup plenty of times," Ochoa volunteered. "Don't worry, Rad! It only hurts the first time! After that I hear you get to like it!"

"And when was your last prostate exam, Rad?" Tshabalala inquired.

The Kong brothers stared at Mrda's rear contact point in a mixture of awe and horror. Haitham turned to Bolan incredulously. "Are all white men so hairy?"

"No, Haitham." Bolan shook his head. "Just Serbs."

Onopkov nodded and contemplated his cigarette. "This is true."

The Kong brothers nodded in unison. "Ah."

"Sure you're not Greek then, Rad?" Ceallach asked.

"Looks like he might swing that way," Tshabalala observed. "He looks awfully comfortable in that position."

"I…will…kill…you…all…." Rad promised.

Russo looked up from her work and regarded Bolan drily. "Would the comedian in chief care to break this up?"

Bolan nodded. "You heard the lady. Show's over, gentlemen."

"Aw, Striker," Ceallach bemoaned. "It was just getting good."

"As soon as Russo is done here have her check your arm and change the bandages." Bolan clicked his com link. "Goose, how's our six look?"

"A lot better than Rad's," Pienaar reported.

Fresh laughter broke out among the assembled soldiers. Bolan suppressed a smile. Despite multiple attempts on them, his team was still salty and ready for anything. "Thank you, Goose."

"Welcome, Striker."

Bolan had a strong suspicion that "anything" was coming, and coming soon. He walked over to Lkhümbengarav. The Mongolian sat on a rock watching the prisoner. The Falcon sniper sat miserably with his hands bound to the Unimog's bumper. He flinched when he suddenly found himself in Bolan's shadow. Lkhümbengarav grinned. "How is the show?"

"Hirsute." Bolan nodded at the Chinese sniper. "Did you get enough to eat?"

The Chinese sniper gave Bolan a wary nod.

"I don't suppose you'd tell me who your commanding officer is?"

The sniper gave Bolan the stone face.

Bolan held up the sniper's radio. "Listen, I think you know that I let the survivors of the night assault go free. All I want to do is parley with whoever is in charge. If you won't tell me your commander's name, just dial the radio to your communications frequency."

The sniper seemed torn.

"I'll let you listen to the conversation." Bolan tilted his head encouragingly. "Afterward, I'll let you go with two canteens of water and two days' worth of your ration packs. Though, I admit that reconstituted cat meat and freeze-dried rice they foist on you boys is pretty heinous. I'll give you two days of our stuff. It's mostly French, not bad."

"My commander will wish to parley with you," the sniper admitted.

"Excellent. Lucky?"

Lkhümbengarav pulled his knife and cut the Falcon's hands free. Bolan held out the radio unit and the sniper adjusted the radio band. The Executioner rose. "Lucky, tie him back up and then set him up a survival pack. T.C.!" Bolan called. "With me!"

The Falcon stiffened where he sat. "You said I could listen!"

Bolan shrugged. "I lied." Ching trotted up and the two warriors walked over to Rover 2 and took a seat beneath the tarp that was stretched over the roll bars.

"Listen and advise?" Ching asked.

"You got it." Bolan clicked to transmit. "Calling Falcon Commander. Repeat. Calling Falcon Commander."

The radio crackled. "This is Falcon Commander. Who is this?"

"Your opponent."

"And?"

"I eliminated your remaining sniper team." Bolan let that sink in for a moment. "The lead sniper was killed. His spotter is alive and unharmed. I intend to release him later in the afternoon when the heat abates. I assume your survivors from the night assault rejoined you?"

"Yes. Your professionalism has been noted. What is it you want?"

"I'm getting tired of kicking your ass. I recommend you turn around and go home. If you try to interfere with me again, I'll be forced to consider a direct counterattack. I told Mnan that if he came any farther south or west I would kill him and every single one of his men. If you and your men are with him, I'll annihilate you."

"You have two options," the Falcon commander stated. "Surrender immediately, and I will see to it that you and your men are not subject to any reprisals from Captain Osmani or Mnan. You will direct me to the objective. Once I have accomplished my mission, I will allow you and your team to take your truck and head for the South Sudanese border.

"Your alternative is to run south as fast as you can. I will not pursue you. You might make it across the South Sudan border. You might even successfully counterattack Mnan and Osmani. This is of no consequence to me.

"However, know this. My government considers the Sudan part of its political, economic and military sphere in Africa. You are not welcome here. If you continue on your present course of action, I cannot guarantee the safety of yourself or any of your surviving men, including the woman. In fact I may be forced to make examples of you." The Falcon commander paused for effect. "Did you know Mnan has a truckload of hyenas with him? He tells stories about them that are almost beyond belief. Yet my intelligence sources can confirm most of them. I suspect yours can, as well. If at any time you wish to surrender, use this radio frequency."

The radio went dead in Bolan's hand. Ching shook his head. "He's coming. He won't stop."

"I know."

"What do you suggest?" Ching asked.

"Gather the team," Bolan said. "It's time we had a talk."

BOLAN PASSED HIS TABLET around. Ceallach whistled at the image of a woman grinning into the camera. "Her name is Dr. Gretchen Bosworth, and she's one of the world's foremost virologists. She used to work for the United States government."

"Used to?" Tshabalala sighed. "Don't much care for the sound of that."

"Uncle Sam helped pay for her graduate studies. She owed him. As a specialist in virology, they put her to work in biowarfare."

Pienaar gave Bolan a suspicious look. "I thought the United States didn't have a biological warfare program."

"We don't. Strictly speaking, our biowarfare research is defensive, working to counter new biological threats that are man-made or that have been lurking in out-of-the-way corners of the world."

"So what's her problem?" Tshabalala asked. "And why is she here?"

Ching spoke quietly. "One of the best ways to find counters to unknown viruses or altered ones that are already known is to invent them yourself."

Bolan nodded. "That's true."

Ochoa spat. "Well…just…shit."

"But like Lucky asked," Ching continued. "Why is she here?"

"She didn't like the program she was on or the direction it was taking. She wanted to work on curing things like AIDS and Ebola instead of concocting end-of-the-world scenarios in her test tubes. When she figured out a way to weaponize smallpox she quit. She was sworn to secrecy on a stack of Bibles and forced to pay back her government loans. The government gave her a new name and a new identity. About two years ago she went AWOL. The CIA got reports that she was working with Doctors Without Borders. The CIA picked up chatter a few weeks ago that some very bad people were circulating Dr. Bosworth's description in some very bad places. They wanted her alive and were willing to pay large for her. We tracked her down to the Sudan. She's changed her name again and is working with volunteer medical teams that move through the refugee camps dispensing aid. We know for a fact that the Russians want her."

Several team members glared at Onopkov. The former Foreign Legionnaire lit a cigarette. "I am a citizen of France."

Bolan smiled at Nelsonne. "We know the French are interested in her, too. Though I would like to believe it's more to keep her out of the wrong hands." Nelsonne smiled back. Bolan glanced west. "We definitely know the PRC wants her."

Tshabalala looked at Pienaar. "It just gets better and better, brother."

"I don't know how many Falcons are behind us," Bolan said. "At least a reinforced squad's worth, plus extras. I figure Osmani has brought about half a platoon and Mnan's got about a hundred men on horses and technicals. Any way you look at it, we have a small army after us, and as I see it we have three choices.

"One, we can surrender. Their commander has said we'll be released once he has Dr. Bosworth. I don't believe him. He'll want to take myself, Russo and definitely T.C. back to Beijing for strenuous, long-term interrogation. My gut tells me that after a short and strenuous on-the-scene interrogation the rest of you will be summarily shot. Though anyone who wants to surrender can stay here and wait for him."

Ceallach raised his good hand. "And the second choice?"

"We cut and run for the south. I'm not doing that, but anyone who wants out can take his or her weapon and food and water. It's bad bush, but you're all soldiers. You've all been in it. You should make it, and with luck most of the bad guys will be following me."

Ching cracked his knuckles. "The third choice, we finish the mission as planned."

"That's the long and short of it. Anyone who wants to surrender or scamper, take the option now." Bolan regarded his team seriously. "Beyond this point all deserters will be shot."

A few nervous laughs met this announcement. Bolan wasn't laughing. No one applied for the first or second choice. "So, Striker," Ching said. "What about this counterattack you were talking about?"

"How about that strongpoint of theirs?" Ceallach suggested. "Booby-trap the back door and we could hold it against a bleeding army. We tear them up until the Janjaweed and Osmani's lads get tired and leave. Then counterattack the Chinamen." He suddenly looked at Ching. "No offense, T.C."

"None taken.

Mrda sat with his undamaged buttock precariously perched on the bumper of Rover 1. "The mission is to extract the woman, not turn the Sudan into Sarajevo."

"Or those rocks into the Alamo." Ochoa nodded toward Mrda. "I'm with pizza butt. I say we grab the bitch and go."

"Pizza butt…"

"Show of hands," Bolan said. "Who's with pizza butt?"

The vote was unanimous. "Good enough. Scotty, you can't load with one arm. You're riding shotgun in the Mog. Haitham, you're with me, Lucky and Sancho in Rover 1. Sancho, teach him how to load the recoilless. Rad, rig yourself a hammock in the back of Mog. Val, help him. Take all the padding you need. It's going to be a rough ride. If it comes to a fight, Rad, you're fighting the Mog's machine gun. T-Lo, refuel the bike and mount up."

The team broke up.

"Russo, walk with me." Bolan headed away from the caravan. A few jealous looks followed him as Russo skipped up beside him. "Anything you want to say to me, Russo?"

"You give good briefing." The French agent grinned.

Bolan snorted. "Anything else?"

"Yes, I do not wish to wait until Bruges."

"I already scrubbed your back."

"Well, bath time is fun time, but you are the kind of man who leaves a woman wanting more," Nelsonne stated.

"So my father taught me. What's your interest in Dr. Bosworth?"

"Whatever do you mean?"

"Why does France want a U.S. biological-warfare expert?" Bolan queried.

"You are aware that the nation of France ratified the Biological and Toxin Weapons Convention of 1984?" Nelsonne countered.

"The nation of France acceded to the BWC. They didn't sign or ratify it."

Nelsonne did a remarkable imitation of a kitten cocking its head and blinking at a sound it didn't recognize.

"You're very good at that," Bolan admitted.

"Thank you, I have spent years perfecting it."

Bolan didn't smile.

"Oh, very well. Could it not be we are aiding our American allies?"

"If that was the case, you would have informed us immediately of everything you knew, rather than signing up for a road trip. You've lost contact with your spy, and you want me to find her for you."

Nelsonne stopped flirting.

"But you want more than just your field agent. Once again, what is the DGSE's interest?"

"I will say this. My government will not allow Dr. Bosworth

to fall into the hands of the PRC or the Sudanese. I am authorized to terminate her before that happens."

"And?"

Nelsonne sighed. "Since joining your team, I have been authorized to allow her to fall into your hands."

"Good to know."

"Is that enough?" she asked.

"It'll have to be."

RAO, OSMANI AND MNAN got together for a meeting. Rao peered at his surviving sniper while Osmani and Mnan bickered. Private 1st Class Hongbo squatted on his heels eating something that was definitely not PRC issue and smelled suspiciously like lamb. Part of Rao wanted to slap it out of the private's mouth. Another part wanted to confiscate it for himself. A third part was suddenly suspicious as to why the enemy had given sniper-spotter Hongbo better rations than the other released prisoners. Rao's first instinct was that the American dog was trying to mess with his mind. However, Rao wasn't the sort of soldier who left these sorts of things to chance. "Tsu!"

Tsu leaped to Rao's side and responded in Mandarin. "Yes, Command Sergeant!"

Rao jerked his head at the unsuspecting sniper and replied in kind. "Debrief Private Hongbo again! With vigor!"

Tsu's brow furrowed as he saw what Hongbo was eating. Tsu strode over and slapped Hongbo off his haunches. Tsu's boots and fresh questions fell on Hongbo like rain. Rao turned back to the war council. It was odd that Mnan was the voice of moderation and Osmani the voice of urgency. Mnan squinted at the beating Hongbo was receiving. "Do you wish me to interrogate him? I assure you, no one can lie to a hyena."

Rao considered the barking, laughing creatures in the truck bed. He had never seen a viler animal in his life. "I will keep your kind offer in mind."

"Anytime." Mnan grinned.

"We need an air strike," Osmani snarled.

Rao reined in his temper. "My government has already lost

a helicopter, an airborne fighting vehicle and nearly a platoon of men. I have been informed that I must complete the mission with the assets I have or that I can muster on my own. Even if my government arranges another strike team it will be days, perhaps a week, before it can be put in place. Your air force has lost two Su-25 fighter jets. They were understandably very upset about this. It has cost my government a great deal in both capital and favors to smooth their feathers. It cost far more to cover up the situation. Unless you have your own contacts in the Sudanese air force that I do not know about, then we shall be without air assets for the duration of the mission."

"I am concerned about where they are going." Mnan traced a gloved finger across the map covering the hood of the Cheetah. "They are heading deeper into the hard country. It really does make one wonder what they're after, and by extension, what it is you are after, Mr. Rao."

Rao scowled and prepared a scathing remark.

Makur suddenly bolted upright. "I think I know where they are going!"

The announcement was met with varying degrees of incredulity. "Oh? Where is that?" Rao asked.

Makur frowned at the map. He was no good at reading them. The Janjaweed were overwhelmingly tribesmen rather than professionally trained soldiers. They navigated by the sun, the stars and the signs of the land as their ancestors had done since ancient times. "I do not know exactly where." Makur sought for the right words. "But I think know what they seek."

Mnan nodded encouragingly. Makur was usually a man of few words. He seemed to be clearly excited by something. "Go on, brother."

"My grandfather told me stories of an oasis, in the hard lands. A place of flowing water and green trees. It was said to be a hidden place, a rest stop for the camel caravans that came out of the Sahara. Of course it has been generations since the time of the caravans. Since the time of the British."

Osmani made a grudging noise. "One hears of such things, but why would he go there?"

"To meet someone," Mnan said, sneering. "Obviously."

"Tsu!" Rao ordered. Tsu ceased his berating of Private Hongbo and ran to Rao's side. "Yes, Command Sergeant!"

"Contact Control, tell them I request satellite imaging of—" Rao calculated time, distance and fuel, and drew a square on the map to the east of their position with a blue pencil "—this area. I am specifically interested in signs of water, anomalous vegetation and signs of habitation."

"Yes, Command Sergeant!"

"Tell them it is Golden Dragon priority."

"Yes, Command Sergeant!"

14

Bolan took Nelsonne aside for a heart-to-heart. "How long ago did you lose contact with your agent tasked to Boswerth?"

"About a week and a half ago. We believe that Dr. Bosworth suspected she was being tracked and decided to go dark. Our first guess is that the doctor confiscated cell phones and laptops. As of our agent's last contact, Dr. Boswerth had six people in her medical team, including our agent."

"Six." The last information Bolan had was Boswerth had been traveling with a single assistant. Four extra doctors could seriously screw up the extraction. "Your agent, as of last contact, her orders are to terminate Boswerth if it looks like she is going to fall into the wrong hands."

"That is correct."

"If you could contact her, can you call her off?" Bolan asked.

"My superiors could. I do not have the authority. However, once I have made contact I assume command of the mission and take the doctor into my custody."

"Interesting that your agent didn't whack her the moment she lost contact."

"What makes you think she hasn't?" Nelsonne asked.

"Because you've deployed with your team. Her priority is to deliver her into your hands and the nation of France, not the United States. I'm still wondering about your nation's interest."

Nelsonne stiffened. "You and I are in the same business. We don't get to pick and choose our missions."

"You and I aren't in the same business, and I choose all my missions."

Nelsonne was quiet for a moment. "That is good work if you can get it."

Bolan had to admit she had him there.

"If it makes you feel any better, as they say in American parlance, 'the jig is up.' I was not lying. Now that an American team—" she smirked at the word *team* "—is on the ground, I am not only authorized to deliver Dr. Bosworth into your custody, but my team and I are ordered to assist in that regard in all ways possible."

"No one in America says 'the jig is up.'"

Nelsonne made a derisive noise. Bolan believed the French agent was telling half the truth. He also believed she was authorized to act in other capacities if opportunities presented themselves, as well as manufacture such opportunities if she could do so without jeopardizing the mission.

"What's your agent's name?" Bolan asked.

Nelsonne smirked again. "Should you ever have the opportunity to speak with her, she will currently answer to the name Pauline LaCoste."

"Thank you."

"You are welcome." Nelsonne glanced at the green glow of her watch. "Time for my shift. Thanks for the talk," she said before sauntering off.

"STRIKER!" TSHABALALA CALLED across the link from his position on point. "Contact!"

Bolan rode shotgun in Rover 1. He clicked his com link. "Convoy, hold position. What have you got, T-Lo?"

"Looks like civilians, Striker, refugees. Scattered like roaches when they saw me. I'm holding off."

"Good work, T-Lo. Hold position. Wave in a friendly fashion but don't approach. I'm coming up."

"Copy that."

"Russo, with me."

Nelsonne slid out of the Mog. She ran up to Rover 1 and

Haitham hauled her up into the back. "Rover 2, Mog. Stay half a klick back." Bolan craned around his seat. "Sancho, load bee-hive."

Ochoa grinned at Haitham. "You heard the man, Haitham!"

Haitham switched out loads in the recoilless attack gun with alacrity and clapped Ochoa on the shoulder. "Ready, Sancho!"

Bolan nodded to Lkhümbengarav. "Take us forward, slow."

Rover 1 rumbled forward. Tshabalala came across the link again. "Striker, be advised of…goats."

"Copy that, T-Lo. Sitrep on refugees."

"Hiding in the rocks and shrubs. Two kids waved back at me. Their mother snatched them fast."

"Goats?"

"The humans bolted one way. The goats went the other."

Bolan brought up his binoculars. Up ahead a black-and-white kid stood shivering and bleating for its mother. "Copy that, T-Lo."

Lkhümbengarav made a noise as though he had come to a decision. "Striker?"

"Yeah, Lucky?"

"I know goats."

"I thought Mongolians knew horses."

"We know horses. We eat goats."

Bolan slid over as the Mongolian hopped out of the Rover. He reached into a bundle of the tenting and pulled out a twenty-six-inch section of fiberglass tent pole. He put a foot on the fender and grabbed some roll bar. The kid stared at the oncoming Land Rover in trembling terror. Lkhümbengarav jumped down and started making shook-shook noises. The kid approached in hopeful hesitation. The Mongolian nodded Bolan onward.

Bolan continued ahead. The trail the refugees and their animals left was clear to see. The Executioner came upon Tshabalala sitting astride his bike. A jumble of rocks and scrub thorn lay in front of him. Bolan pulled to a halt next to his scout. "How many?"

"Two score maybe, Striker."

Bolan hopped out of the Rover. "Haitham, Russo, with me." The big American walked to within fifty yards. He detected some furtive movement behind the hedges of thorn brush. "Haitham, call out."

Haitham waved and shouted a greeting.

"Tell them I'm an American and she's French."

Haitham shouted again. The Sudanese government despised most Western powers. However the citizens in the south and west of the Sudan knew that white people almost always meant food, water and medicine. Lkhümbengarav wandered up, making his Mongolian goat-herding noises. He drove a herd of about twenty goats. His section of tent pole made a reassuring shushing noise in the air above them.

"Haitham," Bolan ordered, "tell them to please come and retrieve their goats."

Haitham called out and waved his arms in mild impatience. A young man came cautiously out of the rocks. He was rail-thin and as dark as the Kong brothers. He looked to be around sixteen or seventeen and wore what appeared to be the tattered remnants of what had once been a school uniform, right down to his ragged shorts and neatly knotted necktie. Incongruously he wore a handmade hat of woven reeds and his feet were wrapped in rags and plastic.

"Haitham, tell him—"

"I speak English," the young man said.

"What's your name?" Bolan asked.

"Shadrach."

"Christian?"

Shadrach gave Bolan a sarcastic look. "How can you tell?"

"Shadrach what?"

"Salva."

"Listen, Mr. Salva—"

"Only my teachers called me Mr. Salva, and they only did it when they were grossly displeased with me." The young man lifted eyes that had held back tears for a long time. "They are all dead."

"Where're you headed, Shaq?"

"Shaq?" Salva brightened. "Like the basketball player?"

"Yeah."

"I am very good at basketball."

"I can tell. Listen, where're you headed, Shaq?"

Salva stifled his pleasure and became reticent.

"Sanctuary is south or west across the border. You're heading due east."

Salva might or might not have been very good at basketball, but he wasn't very good at hiding his thoughts. Bolan decided to go with the truth. He nodded at Nelsonne. "You see the white lady?"

Salva eyed her. "Quite clearly."

"We're looking for another white lady, like her. One who helps refugees." Bolan read Salva's body language. The young man knew exactly who the subject of conversation was. "She is in terrible danger," Bolan finished.

Salva turned and shouted out. "Mesach! Abendengo!" Two boys of about fourteen and twelve came out of the rocks. The elder wore even more ragged school finery than Salva. The younger wore native homespun. They both carried switches and they warily reclaimed their goats from Tshabalala, who smiled at them benevolently. The two Sudanese lads stared at the Mongolian as if he were sporting horns and a tail.

Bolan clicked his com link. "Goose, bring up the convoy." He turned his attention back to Salva. "How many are in your group besides your little brothers?"

"All told, we are forty-two."

"Can you tell us where the lady is?"

"I could."

"You know we could just follow you," Bolan stated.

"You know we could just squat here and eat goats for the next two weeks," Salva countered.

Bolan nodded. "You could do that, but you don't want to meet the people we have behind us."

"Whom do you have behind you?"

"Yellow Mnan."

Salva's eyes bugged out of his head.

"Yeah," Bolan agreed. "It isn't good. He wants the lady. So

does the Sudanese army and some very unreasonable Chinese special forces operatives."

Salva gulped. "Who are you again?"

"Striker."

The youth's eyes widened again. "Do you always bring shit raining down everywhere you go?"

"Usually," Bolan admitted. "But I usually clean up after."

"Fine, I will take you."

"What if you just tell me where she is and I'll pay you," Bolan suggested.

"You are going to pay me anyway, but you are going to take me and my people with you. You do not leave us behind for Mnan."

"I never intended to. How about I pay you, handsomely, and you break south for the South Sudan border. I guarantee you Mnan and his new friends are far more interested in me."

"You cannot guarantee that. You take us with you," Salva argued.

"I can't transport forty people."

Salva pointed at the Mog as it rolled up. "Then you will put the sick and injured in your truck and you will continue at a marching pace."

"You know, Mnan and his friends just might catch up."

"You know, to be honest, I would prefer to have Yellow Mnan and his friends catch up with us with you at our side." Salva lifted his chin defiantly. "And I want twenty thousand U.S. dollars."

"Do I look like I have twenty thousand dollars?"

"Yes."

"You're a hard man, Shaq."

"These are hard times. Do we have a deal?"

"I pay you when you get me to the lady," Bolan stated. "Until then, you and your people will have my protection."

"One other thing."

"What's that?"

"I want a rifle," Salva said.

Bolan turned back to the convoy. "Russo, give Shaq's people a quick medical once-over. Do what you can. Lucky?"

"Yes, Striker?"

"Issue rifles to anyone who applies. Teach them which end is which at our next stop."

"RIDE HARD, BROTHER," Mnan ordered.

"Yes, brother." Makur strung his two remounts behind him. The twenty-man raiding force Mnan had given Makur did the same. Giving each rider two remounts had left the majority of Mnan's men riding on top or in back of the technicals and the Chinese trucks. The horsemen had stripped down for a very hard ride. Besides water, each man carried his rifle, spare magazines and little else. Rao had issued each man two days' worth of his own soldiers' freeze-dried rations to lighten their load. Sergeant Tsu mounted his horse. He was one of the Falcon strike team's ablest riders. In a strange twist of fate so was Private Hongbo. Tsu and the sniper would accompany Makur's raiding force as both intelligence officers and to see to the execution of the PRC's interests. Rao went over the plan a final time. "Satellite imaging has confirmed three possible target areas. We believe the canyon land is the most likely. It is also the farthest. You will proceed there at all speed."

"Yes, Command Sergeant."

Rao switched to Mandarin. "Mnan has given his men strict orders." Rao rolled his eyes. "But dogs such as these cannot be trusted. All Westerners found are to be protected until you are ordered otherwise. The target is to be protected at all costs. You are authorized to kill any or all of Mnan's men if you believe they are endangering the mission."

Rao had issued both Tsu and Hongbo pistols with sound suppressors. Tsu nodded. "Understood."

"You may allow Makur and his men whatever depredations their appetites require among the local inhabitants."

Tsu scowled in disgust but nodded. "Understood, Command Sergeant."

"If you sight the enemy convoy, do not make contact. If you are sighted in return, the only vehicles they have that can follow you are their motorcycles. If they deploy them, pick your spot and have Private Hongbo take them from range."

"Understood."

"I cannot stress it strongly enough that this mission is of national strategic interest to the People's Republic of China."

"Understood."

Rao broke into a rare smile. "Good luck, Comrade Sergeant."

Tsu grunted in amusement. The Chinese military had mostly given up putting the word *comrade* in front of every military ranking. The Communist honorific had been relegated to very formal occasions, though its use rose in frequency the closer one got to Beijing; in corollary, it was also used in black-humor moments the farther one got away from the capital. Rao and Tsu were old-school Falcons. In the past decade they had inserted into some very nasty situations that spanned the PRC's Asian sphere interests from Vietnam to India. "I will, Comrade Command Sergeant."

"Comrade Sergeant?"

"Yes, Comrade Command Sergeant?"

"Ride hard."

Tsu saluted and looked at Makur, who nodded and spurred his horse. Sergeant Tsu and the Janjaweed rode west.

15

The brothers Shadrach, Mesach and Abendengo turned out to be the refugee band's sole fighting force, and they were armed with sticks. The rest were women and children. All the males over the age of fourteen had been killed. The boys and girls between the ages of ten and thirteen had been enlisted as child soldiers and concubines. Slavery was the destination of the women of childbearing age. Shadrach and Mesach had survived the destruction of their school and returned to their village to find Abendengo huddled with the survivors who had escaped the carnage. Among the refugees, the Lady of the Oasis was a desperate survival dream.

Lkhümbengarav stood over the brothers as they shot. During the food and refueling break, he had given the three young men an intensive course in firing and maintaining an assault rifle. He had retained his tent-pole section like a baton of office. The Mongolian wasn't above lashing out with it when unforgivable failures of the manual of arms manifested themselves. It wasn't a school of firearms instruction Bolan subscribed to, but it seemed to be working. The stubby, Chinese QBZ-95 bullpup assault rifles the team had looted from the Falcon airborne assault each mounted a 4-power scope. It was thirty minutes since the lesson had begun, and the Salva brothers were all reliably putting rounds into an empty fuel drum at fifty yards. Bolan nodded to himself.

It would do.

It would have to.

"Lucky!" Bolan called.

"Cease fire!" the Mongolian bawled. "Yes, Striker?"

"Let them eat and then let's get on the road!"

"You heard the man!" Lkhümbengarav shouted. "Strip your weapons like I showed you! Clean your weapons like I showed you! Lock and load and get your chow!" He tapped his fiberglass wand into his palm. "You have twenty minutes!"

Shaq gaped in shock. "Sergeant Lucky, we—"

"Fifteen minutes!" the man snarled.

The Salva brothers gasped and sucked their fingers as they fieldstripped their smoking-hot rifles. The Mongolian stomped past. "Lucky," Bolan said.

"What!"

"Little rough?"

He glared up at Bolan. "You're giving me just enough time to teach those boys to die fighting and going forward. You don't like my methods? Fuck you, hot rod."

"We came on Shaq and his people by chance, Lucky. Should I have had Val torture the doctor's location from them and moved on, leaving them for Mnan?"

Lkhümbengarav glared but had no prepared response.

"You had your chance to bug out yesterday. But what the hell, Lucky. I'll give you a second chance. Take one of the Chinese motorcycles out of the back of the Mog and go. Go now."

The Mongolian ground his teeth. "Is there anything else?"

"Yeah, one more thing."

"What's that?"

"The next time you say 'fuck you' to me in public, I will publicly kick your teeth down your throat."

Lkhümbengarav's features slowly relaxed, and a slow smile spread across his face.

"I would like to publicly say that I'm excited about this plan. I'm thankful to be a part of it. Let's do this."

Bolan nodded. "Drill them again at our next stop. Meantime, I want Shaq in Rover 1 with me, and you, Mesach and Abendengo walking with their people."

"Copy that, Striker."

Bolan walked over to the Mog and stepped up on the back

bumper to peer in the back. Old women, the injured and sick and children sat spread around between supplies and ordnance. Mrda lay in his hammock. Three Sudanese children were piled on top of him. He met Bolan's gaze and sighed like a male lion beset by cubs.

"How you doing, Rad?"

"My ass hurts," he replied. "And for famine victims, these children weigh like lead."

"You're a good man, Rad."

"Fuck you, Striker. I heard what you said to Lucky. Go ahead, do your worst."

"You're wounded, Rad. You have privileges. Say anything you want. Of course I'm the only one who has access to the codeine."

"We have codeine?"

"And morphine, but in short supply and saved for the polite and the deserving."

The little girl wadded up on Mrda's chest tugged at his week-old beard and looked at Bolan. "He is very hairy."

"He's a Serb."

The little Sudanese girl nodded in acceptance of that fact and curled back up. Mrda glared at the metal roof of the Mog's cargo container. "Is there anything else, Striker?"

"Yeah, I think the fight is coming soon. You think you can fight?"

"Give me my rifle, put me in the position you think best. I will fight. I will shoot. We will win."

Bolan nodded as he hopped off the Mog's back bumper.

Ochoa handed Bolan a cup of coffee. "Thanks."

"You're welcome."

Bolan gulped the coffee gratefully. He realized he was more tired than he thought. "How you doing, Sancho?"

"I'm cool." Ochoa leaned close. "Shit's coming down, ain't it, Striker?"

"Yeah, it's all coming to a head."

Bolan's phone buzzed on cue. "What do you have, Bear?"

"I have a possible location."

The Executioner watched as his phone's screen turned into

a satellite map. A tiny green *x* marked the position of the convoy in another stretch of scrub and thorn. To the east and north a similar red *x* marked a maze of canyon land. "Not too far," Bolan said. "But not where I would have suspected. Can you get me higher resolution?"

"Not until tomorrow, but there are anomalies. The satellite that mapped the area couldn't look down into the section of canyons." Kurtzman increased the gain. "What does it look like to you?"

What Bolan saw in the satellite picture looked vaguely like a starfish. The hard rocks of the low hills and canyons were cut by a five-armed mass that defied description and barely filled a square kilometer. Bolan had seen satellite similar photos but not in this configuration.

"It's an oasis," Ochoa said.

"Very good," Bolan acknowledged.

"I'm from Mexico, *Jefe*." Ochoa grinned. "We know something about secret canyons."

"The canyons were cut by water aeons ago, but the water that's still there is in wells and water table," Bolan said. "They've strung camouflage netting through the palm trees. It's a camp."

"That's the way we figure it on our end," Kurtzman said. "We picked up the anomaly from yesterday's grid-by-grid. Most observers, well, hell, most observers wouldn't have a satellite looking at that little nook of the Sudan, and most wouldn't have thought twice about it much less had the satellite gain to give it a closer look. I'm juggling satellites, but I'll bet you anything if I can get eyes on tonight I'll have the heat signatures of campfires."

"I'll take that bet, Bear."

"Figured you'd say that. By tomorrow we should—"

"I'm putting eyes on it tonight, Bear."

Kurtzman heaved a sigh. "I figured you were going to say that, too."

"And if the target is there, I intend to lay my hands on it. Bear, once the target is acquired, I'm going to break hard south for the border. If we hit trouble, it's going to be a hundred-mile fighting retreat. Have Jack ready to go. He takes Boswerth and her team first. If the LZ becomes hot or the Sudanese air force reacts, my team and I will escape and evade, and then advise."

"Does your team know that?" Kurtzman asked.

Bolan glanced at Ochoa. The Ranger grinned back. "They suspect."

"Very well, Striker. Positioning *Dragonslayer* to a refugee camp within range behind the South Sudanese border. She will be fueled, fully armed and hot on the pad within four hours."

Bolan looked at the swiftly sinking sun. "That'll do just fine, Bear. Striker out."

Ochoa shook his head. "You said it was coming down. Looks like it's coming down tonight."

Bolan called out. "T-Lo! Got a job for you!"

Tshabalala finished the last of his coffee, scooped up his rifle and trotted over. "Striker?"

Bolan pulled his tablet out of his hip sack and synced it. He held out the tablet and the satellite image on it to his best scout. "I need you to go here, tonight, as fast as you can and give me a recon."

Tshabalala looked at the satellite map and gauged it like a pro. "I'll go by bike for the first twenty klicks. Last ten I'll run."

Bolan nodded. "Go now."

The scout grabbed two canteens from the supply table and threw a leg over his bike. The rest of the team watched as the South African tore out of camp with the sun setting behind him. It said something about the professionalism of Bolan's team that no one asked any questions. The team finished its coffee and chow, then began moving toward their personal pile of weapons and gear for the final check of their equipment. Bolan looked at the satellite image on his tablet again.

He knew tonight was the night.

BOLAN STARED UPWARD. If the Sudan had a saving grace, it was that there was so little light pollution that the cloudless night sky was nothing short of spectacular. He looked down at his watch and gauged the time and distance of Tshabalala's journey. The bike ride could be measured in minutes. The canyon creep Bolan had ordered would take hours. He wasn't surprised as the Mongolian's voice came across the link in a hiss. The South African scout didn't sound happy.

"Contact, Striker."

"Sitrep."

"It's bad."

A cold feeling in Bolan's guts had told him it would be.

"Target area has been compromised. Target compromised. Jesus…I have between…fifteen and twenty hostiles."

"I need a number, T-Lo. Count the horses."

"Right!" He came back in about three heartbeats. "I have twenty-two horses being minded by two hostiles. Hostiles seem to be mostly Janjaweed. I see two Falcons."

"Target status?"

"I see the target and peripherals. They've lined everyone up including the locals…" His voice sounded strained. "I think things are going to be done."

Bolan's blood went cold. "Copy that, T-Lo. Putting you on speaker phone." The Executioner walked over to the equipment table. His team was formed up and ready to go whatever the mission. Bolan picked up his sound-suppressor tube and spun it onto the end of his Beretta 93-R machine pistol. He swapped out his magazine of hollowpoint rounds for one of subsonic ammunition. He had already snapped down the folding foregrip and installed the laser designator. The high-frequency infrared laser was invisible to the human eye but would paint a star-bright point of brilliance onto his target in the view of his night-vision goggles.

Bolan clicked the detachable metal stock into the grip and turned his pistol into a carbine. "I want to go in surgical. T.C., Lucky, you're coming with me. We're Team 1."

Ching gazed at the Beretta admiringly. "We only have one silenced weapon, Striker."

Bolan cocked his head. "I thought you were a silenced weapon."

Laughter broke out among the warriors. Ching smiled and held up a well-callused right hand with his fingers in the tiger-claw formation. "In all modesty, it is not the first time that has been said."

Bolan let the cheers and comments about what Ching's right hand was capable of run their course. "Our first and foremost is to secure Dr. Bosworth. If possible, our secondary objective is to secure Russo's agent and the rest of the medical staff. My pistol is quiet but it's not silent. T.C., you're taking out the closest sentry on our vector. Lucky and I are going straight for the hostages. While we do that, you clean the perimeter of the rest of the sentries. If we run into trouble you come in hard, fast and firing."

"Copy that."

"Russo and Val are Team 2. Goose, you're going to link up with T-Lo and be Team 3. You're fire support from above, only come in if I call. You copy that, T-Lo?"

Tshabalala came back over the speaker. "Copy that, Striker."

"Sancho, you're Team 4 with Haitham and Shartai. Hang back on the extraction route. If we come on the run, you three are defending the extraction. Load rifle grenades. Scotty and Rad are going to defend the convoy with the Salva brothers while we're gone, but Scotty I want you to keep Rover 2 warmed up. If I call for it, I want you to advance and take out enemy pursuit with the fifty."

Bolan looked around his team. "Everyone know their job?"

Everyone did.

"Let's do it."

16

Bolan heard moans and wails of desolation as he approached Tshabalala's position. He was grateful that it hadn't transitioned into the screams of the tortured and dying. Ching's knuckles popped and crackled as he clenched his hand into a killing weapon. Bolan spoke softly into his com. "T-Lo, Team 1 on your six."

"Come ahead, Team 1," the South African responded.

Bolan and his men moved upslope to the lip of the canyon wall. It was as he had predicted. The starfish shape he had seen on satellite was an oasis, with three wells in the middle. The few ancient clay-brick buildings surrounding them were in disrepair but had been modified and reroofed with tarps, plastic sheeting and various pieces of flotsam and jetsam. Tents, lean-tos and shelter halves lay scattered beneath the canopy of the palm trees. Goats and chickens shell-shocked from the sudden attack by the raiders wandered aimlessly.

The soldier counted about two hundred refugees, which had been divided into four groups. Old men and women made up one pool and perhaps they were the luckiest. Bolan suspected they had been culled out for death. Their silent, dead eyes spoke volumes. The next group consisted of women of childbearing age. They were roped together in a coffle. The next group was a small handful of able-bodied men. Several were wounded and all badly beaten. They were individually bound, and wept and cursed in impotent rage and despair. The next group were the young ones ranging from teens to toddlers. They huddled among themselves moaning and crying.

"Target is in the middle building," Ching whispered.

The ancient little brick house had rusted corrugated tin for a roof. In the firelight Bolan saw two men in Western garb sitting cross-legged and miserable against the wall with their hands tied behind them. One of the Falcons guarded the door.

"You've seen the doctor?" Bolan asked.

"Yeah, she and Russo's friend were allowed out about half an hour ago to relieve themselves," Ching replied. "I think the Falcons and the Janjaweed commander are trying to keep a lid on things until the Chinese commander arrives to pick up the doctor." He jerked his chin at a huge individual who was clearly in authority. "The big one slapped around two of his men he caught dragging one of the women into the trees. I think they're worried about the orgy getting out of hand."

Tshabalala scowled through his optics. "Looks like some of the boys are getting very tired of waiting."

Bolan scanned the captives' dwelling again. A good section of the tin roof had rusted away and been replaced by plastic. "Any guards inside?"

"The head Falcon, and a Janjaweed. It looked like they brought them some food a few minutes ago."

Bolan nodded and clicked his com link. "Scotty, sitrep on the convoy."

"All quiet, Striker. Refugees fed, rested and ready to move. Got Shaq up on the hill with a pair of night goggles."

"Shaq," Bolan said over the com link. "How you doing?"

The young man came back eagerly. His pride in being part of the team was infectious. "Watching our back trail, Striker. Nothing to see."

"Do me a favor, Shaq."

"What is that?"

"Keep an eye north," Bolan directed him.

"I will, Striker!"

"All units, Lucky and I are going behind the hostage building and in through the top. Team 2, sitrep."

"In position, northern canyon branch. Have eyes on objective."

"Copy that." Bolan ran his optics past the dwelling the captives inhabited. Two very bored-looking Janjaweed thugs stood smoking cigarettes and frequently glancing back toward the campfires and the refugees. "Team 1, going in."

Bolan slipped away from Tshabalala and Pienaar's position on the canyon lip. Ching and Lkhümbengarav followed as silent as shadows. The men threaded their way through the maze of rock guided by the images Kurtzman had sent. They doubled back along a ravine, following the sound of misery, and found themselves on the outskirts of the southern end of the oasis. The two guards stood as plain as day in Bolan's night-vision gear. The guards kept doing Bolan a favor by staring back toward the campfire and ruining their eyes' natural adaption to the dark. "T.C., you think you can take both?"

"Can I take both..." Ching moved forward shaking his head. He took out the two sentries before they knew what hit them. His right hand hit the closer sentry between the eyes like the bolt from a cattle gun, and the man dropped to the ground. Ching's fist opened into a knife-hand configuration and snapped into the second sentry's throat. He instantly covered the sentry's mouth and pinched his nose shut while easing him to dust. The sentry kicked feebly as he swallowed bits of his broken esophagus and lay still. Ching unslung his rifle and gave Bolan the thumbs-up.

"Sentries eliminated," Bolan reported. "Team 1 taking objective. All units stand ready." He and Lkhümbengarav moved at a crouch through the dark. They linked up with Ching and took up position behind the dwelling. Ching assumed the position against the wall and Bolan clambered onto his shoulders. A gap in the plastic sheeting revealed the interior. Dr. Bosworth was sitting in the far corner. The doctors and assistants sat lined up along the wall. All were bound. The Janjaweed sentry wore homespun and an ancient-looking French flak jacket, and held a watery-looking bowl of some kind of gruel and goat's milk. He had dropped to a knee in front of the French-Canadian agent and had tipped the bowl to her lips. Most of the prisoners had milk mustaches. He allowed the agent three swallows and moved down the line to an African man in khaki and let him have a few swallows.

Bolan nodded to himself.

From his vantage he saw that the woman had a razor blade in her hands, and had returned to very slowly sawing at her bonds the moment her captor had moved down the line. The Falcon sat in the corner opposite Dr. Bosworth with a clear line of fire on the open doorway. His assault rifle lay across his knees, and he was rapidly chopsticking some kind of glutinous mass out of a steaming foil pouch into his mouth. Bolan gave Lkhümbengarav a hand signal for a diversion, and the man palmed a small stone. The big American raised his Beretta. The Mongolian wound up and unerring beaned a billy goat. The animal rose on its back legs and bleated in outrage. The nannies and kids around it bleated and scattered. Bolan's pistol coughed. The Falcon's head jerked in answer to the subsonic bullet and he sagged, spilling his dinner in his lap. The Janjaweed guard looked up and Bolan's pistol coughed twice in rapid succession. The guard flopped backward out of his squat and spilled the gruel all over himself.

Bolan's knife slid through the plastic like butter and he dropped down among the captives. "This is a rescue. I need silence. Stay out of view of the doorway." He scooped up the dead Falcon's rifle and held it out to the Canadian. "Agent LaCoste."

Pauline LaCoste brought her hands in front of her, trailing the severed rope. Dr. Bosworth glared at her erstwhile assistant but kept silent. Ching swiftly cut the prisoners' bonds. He finished freeing Bosworth and pressed the fallen Janjaweed thug's Kalashnikov into her hands. She looked at the rifle long and hard, then checked the weapon and held it at the ready.

Bolan nodded at Ching. "Do it."

Ching moved to one side of the door and called out softly in Mandarin. A familiar face stepped around the doorjamb bearing a long-barreled Type 95 rifle in designated marksman configuration. Ching yanked the Falcon inside and put him into a stranglehold. As Lkhümbengarav took the Falcon's weapon away from him, Bolan pointed his Beretta between the sniper's eyes. "Private Hongbo, isn't it? Blink once for yes and twice for no."

Hongbo blinked once.

"Listen, I told your commander after our last dustup I wasn't taking any prisoners."

Hongbo's eyes bugged in response.

"You want to live."

Hongbo blinked in the affirmative.

Bolan nodded at Ching and the warrior eased his grip on Hongbo's neck slightly. He shifted his hands from the stranglehold to the neck-snap position. Hongbo flinched helplessly. He tried to step backward as Bolan loomed in, but Ching left him nowhere to go.

"What's your commander's name?"

"Rao."

"You guys pulled an end run on horseback to get here ahead of us. How did you know the oasis was here?"

"The large one, Makur. He said he had heard rumors of such a place. Knowing what we were looking for made satellite confirmation fairly easy."

"Where are the rest of your people?" Bolan asked.

"They no longer follow your convoy."

"They're sweeping north, taking the same trail the horses took?"

Hongbo gulped. "Yes, the technicals cannot do it by night, but the SUVs using night-vision gear can follow the route through the bush and cut straight into the canyons. We have left markers."

"How long ago did you contact Rao?" Bolan prompted.

"We took the oasis at sunset. We radioed in once it was secure. We check in on the half hour."

"When is the next half hour?"

Hongbo hesitated.

"I like you, Hongbo." Bolan pushed his selector to 3-round-burst mode. "I like a marksman. I really want you to get this right."

Hongbo looked unhappily at his fellow Falcon slumped against the wall with subsonic hollowpoint rounds bisecting his brainpan. "Sergeant Tsu was in charge of this. But my best guess is within minutes."

"Hongbo, if you don't screw this up, sniper to sniper, I'll let you live." Bolan turned to Lkhümbengarav. "Go over the top. T.C, help the civilians over the wall. We link up with the convoy and head hard south."

Bolan touched his phone. "Bear, targets acquired. We're going to break hard south to get out of the canyons. Find me some kind of defensible LZ. It's going to take two trips to bring out the civilians and the team."

"On it, Striker."

Dr. Bosworth sighed. "There's a problem with that plan."

"Make it fast," Bolan said.

She pointed her rifle at Bolan's chest. "I'm not going anywhere."

Bolan met the doctor's eyes. They were as steady as the muzzle of her weapon. "Gretzky, we don't have time for this."

The doctor blinked. "How did you—" Her eyes narrowed. "You have a file on me."

"I can pretty much get files on anyone I want." Bolan shrugged. "I'm that guy."

Bosworth kept her rifle on Bolan but glared at Hongbo. "So this asshole's friends, and an army of Janjaweed, are coming."

"And about two squads of Sudanese regulars," Bolan confirmed.

"And you expect me to leave nearly two hundred refugees, mostly women, children and seniors for them? You expect a doctor to abandon her patients?"

Bolan locked eyes with the doctor. "Gretzky, I kid you not. This isn't the first time I've been in a situation like this. My heart is breaking."

"I believe you."

"But I only have one helicopter, and it's got to make two trips just for your team and mine."

"So wipe these guys out."

"I don't have the time or the ammo. Chinese special forces are on their way. Sudanese army is on its way. Yellow Mnan is on his way."

Bosworth started at the name. "All the more reason."

"Do you mind if I call you Gretzky?"

"Not at all, all my friends do."

"You're not going to shoot me."

Boswerth slowly nodded. "You're right." She slowly raised her muzzle toward the plastic over her head. "I'm counting to five. You'd better bring your people in."

Bolan grimaced. "T.C.?" Private Hongbo managed several guttural clicking sounds as he suddenly found himself being choked out.

The big American shook his head at the woman. "Don't do this."

"You know you want me to."

"Part of me, definitely, yeah. But if this is how it has to go down, let me do it my way."

"I would, but you and I just don't have that reservoir of trust yet." Boswerth squeezed her trigger and her AK blasted five rounds through the roof.

Bolan snarled across the link. "All units! Engage!"

Pienaar and Tshabalala's rifles cracked into life instantly. Bolan stepped to the doorway. "Lucky! T.C.! Get them out of here! LaCoste! With me!"

Two Janjaweed thugs were running straight for the house. Bolan drilled a 3-round burst into both of them center body mass. The South Africans had already dropped six hostiles. Bolan took a knee and shot two more. LaCoste leaned around the door and fired. A Janjaweed terrorist running toward the horses fell. Four hostiles had made it to the corral and mounted. Nelsonne and Onopkov opened up and bullet-riddled men sagged from their saddles as the horses screamed and bucked. "I've count seventeen down! I'm missing five!"

"I have two running down the northern canyon branch," Ching responded. "You want me to take them?"

"Go!"

A grenade landed on top of the plastic over their heads and its weight let it slide down the tarp toward the hole Bolan had cut. LaCoste snarled. *"Merde!"*

Bolan shoulder-rolled across the floor and snapped up his

weapon. His first burst lifted the grenade off the tarp and the second sent it skittering toward the southern side, away from refugees and hostages. The grenade detonated with a thud and dust oozed out of the ancient brick wall. The soldier slapped down his night-vision goggles and strode outside. Two men stood plainly beneath the palms a dozen yards away. Bolan printed a burst through the chest of one and then the other. He knelt and scanned. "All units! Cease fire! I count twenty down! Anyone hurt?"

No one was.

Ching's voice came across the link. "Make that twenty-two."

"Copy that, Striker!" Pienaar replied. "Then I count twenty-two down."

"Roger," Tshabalala confirmed. "Verified."

"Lucky?"

"I have the doctors at the first bend in the ravine, holding position."

Bolan rose and walked back to the ruins. Hongbo lay gasping like a fish. The Executioner pointed his smoking machine pistol between his eyes again. "You came here with twenty-two. "

"Yes!" Hongbo gasped.

"No one rode double? You don't have a motorcycle or two parked out in the maze?"

"No…"

"I believe you." Bolan took a long breath. "Lucky, bring Gretzky and her people back. T.C., join up. Sancho, bring up Rover 2 and take defensive position on the northern canyon branch."

Everyone came back in the affirmative.

Ceallach came across the link. "And the convoy, Striker?"

"Bring everybody in, Scotty." Bolan braced himself for the storm to come and touched his phone. "Bear, this is Striker."

"Sitrep."

"Boswerth and her team secure. Refugees secure. Oasis secured."

"Copy that. Bring up the convoy and proceed to—"

"Negative, Bear."

This wasn't the first time Bolan had presented Kurtzman with this situation, and the computer expert recognized it immediately. "Tell me you're not doing this, and then please tell me what we're supposed to tell the President."

"It's fluid. I'm going to have to get back to you. How soon do you have eyes on?"

"Four hours to our next window, Striker." Kurtzman sighed. "Should I send in Jack?"

"No place for him to land."

"He could winch up Dr. Bosworth and her team. Then the mission would be accomplished, and you can play Magnificent Seven to your heart's content."

"Don't be that guy, Bear."

"I'm paid to be that guy!"

"Yeah, well, I have to go talk to my team."

17

Bolan finished his pitch. "So who's in?"

The small sea of faces arranged in front of him stared back with varying degrees of enraged wonder. Ceallach spoke first. "Didn't I tell you I've seen this movie on the telly, Striker? Everyone bloody dies!"

Murmurs and snarls of agreement met this statement. The larger arc of refugees behind cringed as the warriors heated up.

Lkhümbengarav stabbed out a finger. "Did I mention you fascinate me, GI?"

Mrda spit. "For fuck's sake, Striker!"

"Striker," Onopkov said, shaking his head slowly. "No."

Ochoa began walking in circles and waving his arms. "Would someone please talk sense to him? Better yet, T.C., would you just hit him and pack him in the Mog so we can all get out of here and go home?"

Ching seemed to be considering the prospect.

Haitham raised his hand.

Bolan nodded. "Haitham?"

"We're in."

Pienaar rolled his eyes. "Oh, for—"

Shartai rose. The young scout's jaw set determinedly. "Yellow Mnan must die." The Kong brothers crossed an invisible line to stand beside Bolan.

LaCoste looked at Nelsonne. "This is absolutely outside the mission profile."

"You know—" the doctor pointed a finger at LaCoste "—you

need to sit down and have yourself a long tall glass of shut the fuck up, traitor bitch."

"Traitor?" LaCoste wrinkled her nose. "I am completely loyal to Quebec and the nation of France."

The three Salva brothers rose without a word and fell in behind Bolan.

Tshabalala gestured to encompass Bolan and his five recruits. "You think you and your Sudanese teen commandoes are going to make a bit of difference? Here?"

"Yeah, I do."

"Agent Nelsonne," LaCoste repeated. "This is outside the mission profile."

"Our mission remains the same. Dr. Bosworth is now in American custody. As long as she is in the Sudan our mission is to protect her, or terminate her if it looks like she is going to fall into enemy hands," Nelsonne concluded. "We are in."

Bosworth considered the assault rifles in the two agents' hands. "Um…thanks?"

LaCoste's eyes narrowed at her superior. "I will allow you to explain this to the director."

Bolan raised his voice for all to hear. "LaCoste is right. This is totally outside the mission profile. I know what I said at the last stop, so just consider this checkpoint two. Anyone who wants to leave, go ahead. If there are enough of you who want to go, you can have the Mog, but you're leaving the weapons and all the supplies, except for your personals and what you need to reach the South Sudan border, here with me. Once you are back in the world my people will contact you and give you the second half of your pay."

Glares and stony silence met the announcement.

Nelsonne turned to her team. "You have my permission to leave." LaCoste swore in French. Nelsonne ignored her. "Once you are in Bruges, you will be able to pick up your pay from the nation of France, as well."

Onopkov and Mrda looked at each other. The Russian shrugged. "Then I leave."

Mrda shook his head at the Russian. "I stay with Russo."

"I leave," Onopkov repeated.

Ceallach nodded. "Too bloody right, Val! And I will take you up on the Mog, Striker." The Briton turned to the rest of the team. "Anyone who—"

"Anyone who stays and fights, and survives?" Bolan interrupted. "I'll triple your pay."

Angry stares went slack into simply staring.

Ochoa's jaw dropped. "Triple…"

"Rao, Osmani and Mnan are on their way. I need you all to make your decision quick so I can start making plans for them based on who and what I have."

Ochoa nodded. "I'm down."

"You sure?"

"For triple? I'm down with you all day in every way, *Jefe.*"

Onopkov stared at Bolan like a man considering drawing on an inside straight. He blew a long stream of smoke and sighed as temptation got the better of him. "Very well."

"The boys back in Ulan Bator—" Lkhümbengarav shook his head in wonder "—are never going to believe this." The Mongolian turned to Ching. "T.C.?"

Ching inclined his head in the affirmative. "I know of this Rao. I would like to see him dead."

Tshabalala looked at his brother-in-law. "My wife is never going to forgive me for this."

Pienaar gave him a wry look. "Mine, neither." He turned to Bolan. "We're in, china."

Everyone looked at Ceallach, who deflated before the peer pressure. "Aw, hell, then…"

MNAN AND OSMANI FROWNED mightily as they stood around the folding command table. Rao shook his head and put away his radio. "My men do not respond."

Mnan gazed eastward. "I fear Makur is dead. What do your eyes in the sky tell you, Rao?"

"The Yankee and his team do not seem to have moved," Rao said. "Nor have the refugees."

"The American commando and his team do not wish to be

caught out in the open," Mnan declared. "Much less with hundreds of refugees to defend."

"That is the way I see it," Rao agreed. The veteran Falcon considered his options. They weren't good. "Time is on their side. We are running low on fuel, as well as water. If we do not act soon, we will have to start cannibalizing fuel and abandoning vehicles. It is very likely that one or two of the American's team are smuggling out Dr. Bosworth on foot or horseback undetected through the canyons, and every moment of our pursuit increases our risk of exposure."

Mnan let his breath out between his teeth as he looked at Rao's map. The vast majority of the map was nearly featureless scrub with the rare bump of hills barely worth noting geographically. To the east was the red *x* that Rao had drawn to mark the oasis, and that mark sat in a furious set of squiggles that represented the canyon land. "I do not relish going into that maze and trying to dig the American and his team out. To be honest I believe it would be a battle we would stand a very good chance of losing."

Rao had to agree. The twisting, walled terrain would be one long string of ambushes that the SUV and technicals couldn't survive. Snipers, booby traps and ambushes would eat up their numerical advantage in manpower. Rao looked back and forth between Osmani and Mnan. "My orders require me to try. I cannot compel you to join me. Should we win, I can increase you compensation dramatically."

"I want the blue-eyed devil dead more than anything I have desired in some time." Mnan gazed eastward again. "But dead men do not reap vengeance, much less live to spend remuneration, no matter how dramatic."

Osmani gazed long and hard upon Rao's map. "Kiir!" Osmani snapped his fingers. "Kiir! Bring me my map!" Kiir scampered forward and laid out Osmani's military map of the area. The captain took a blue pencil and marked their current position and the oasis. "We are here, they are there."

"Thank you for reestablishing that, Captain," Mnan said drily.

The fact that Osmani didn't react to the insult told Rao that the captain was on to something. "And?"

A thin ugly smile crossed Osmani's lips as he tapped a black dot on the map. The dot was north and nearly exactly equidistant between the two blue x's. "Camp Abdel is here."

Rao shook his head. "I am very worried about increasing our exposure. You, yourself, are effectively AWOL from your station and your duties. Calling for assistance from your military very well might cause far more problems than it would solve. It would require explanations about very sensitive matters. In fact it could jeopardize the whole operation."

"In that regard we have an advantage."

"What advantage is that?" Rao inquired.

"We have Major Akeel."

Mnan burst out laughing.

Rao raised a wary eyebrow. "Is he good?"

"Akeel? Rahim Akeel?" Mnan laughed again. "Akeel is a bumbling idiot!"

Rao frowned.

Osmani was undeterred. "Mnan is right. Major Akeel is an incompetent. He spent most of his time during the war embarrassing the government by slaughtering civilians. In his two major engagements with the southern rebels he was beaten decisively. Indeed he most likely would have been stripped of his rank and shot except for the importance of the Akeel family in Khartoum. He is currently stationed at Camp Abdel, out here, specifically as punishment and to keep him out of the way."

Rao looked at Osmani steadily. "This is to our advantage?"

"It is exactly to our advantage. Major Akeel is a bumbling idiot, a laughingstock who would do anything to redeem himself and return to Khartoum and rise to the rank of general."

Rao saw it. "And you propose…?"

"I propose that Major Akeel might take some of his forces out on maneuvers, which is his prerogative. He might just find evidence of rebel activity in the canyon lands and investigate. Rather than alerting the rebels with radio chatter and giving them the chance to escape, he cleverly seeks assistance from a militia leader who happens to be in range."

Mnan smiled.

"That militia leader," Osmani continued, "happens to be working with military advisers from our great ally the People's Republic of China. Together, in a combined arms operation, they destroy the rebel base in a smashing victory."

Rao calculated. "The story is a bit long, and thin."

Osmani waved a dismissing hand. "We will have dozens of bodies, caches of weapons and, may I add, the bodies of genuine foreign mercenaries operating on Sudanese soil. That, and your government putting some money in the right hands, should solve any problems."

Mnan stared at Osmani grudgingly. "This could work."

"Do you know this Major Akeel?"

"Yes, we went to military academy together. In fact he owes me some favors, and I believe he will jump at this opportunity," Osmani replied.

"Does he have any planes?"

"No."

"Gunships?"

"No," the captain repeated.

"Helicopters of any sort?"

"None."

"What *does* he have?" Rao asked.

Captain Osmani smiled.

"STRIKER, THEY HAVE TANKS," Kurtzman said.

"Define *tank,* Bear."

"Like tank-tanks, and they are definitely heading your way," the computer wizard said.

"They have bloody fucking tanks!" Ceallach bellowed.

Bolan idly considered kneecapping the man. "Thank you, Scotty."

"Well, you're welcome, I'm sure."

"How many and what kind, Bear?"

"Two platoons, given the Sudanese inventory and where they rolled out of, I am calling them Chinese Type 69s supplied by a Major Akeel."

"Give me more," Bolan demanded.

"They're your basic Soviet-era T-55 with some upgrades."

"Reactive armor? Night vision?"

"I doubt it, given the godforsaken base they rolled out of, this is some of the Sudanese army's second- or third-line stuff. I'm sending you specs."

"Copy that. How about infantry?"

"Three truckloads."

"Trucks?" Bolan questioned. "No infantry fighting vehicles or armored personnel carriers?"

"That's the blessing if there is one. They have three flatbeds full of men, but I do mean full. The trucks are struggling to keep up with the tanks. I'd say you have a day, given that the Falcons are the only ones with any night-vision gear. You're most likely looking at a daylight attack. Satellite imaging confirms that Rao, Osmani, Mnan and the boys are moving to link up with them."

"Thanks, Bear. Keep me advised. Striker out."

Ceallach glared. "Bloody fucking tanks."

"Yeah." Bolan shrugged. "But they're not very good tanks." He called out across the camp. "Lucky! You know anything about Type 69 tanks?"

The Mongolian looked up from his weapon inventory and grinned. "We use them!"

"And?"

"They suck!"

Bolan held up his rifle. "Suck enough for rifle grenades?"

"Type 69 is old-school, hot rod! Rolled-steel armor! An anti-armor grenade could take it from the top, maybe the sides."

"They have eight tanks, three trucks, six armored SUVs and three technicals. What do we have left in our larder?" Bolan asked as he joined him.

"Well, the good news is after our loot and spoils from fighting Osmani, Mnan and then the Falcons, we have more rifles and ammo than we know what to do with."

Team members began gathering around and listening intently.

"I need to bust up tanks, armored SUVs and technicals, Lucky."

"We have four standard rounds left for the recoilless. Those

crack a Type 69 no sweat, but we cannot afford to exchange. We
also have two beehive and two illumination rounds. We have
two antiarmor rifle grenades left. The rest are frags. We have
two RPGs each, with a reload. Those may or may not crack a
Type 69 frontal. We have the mortar but only three rounds for
it. We have the grenade launcher. I suggest dismounting it. We
have two antitank hand grenades from the Falcons, but someone is going to have to stand up and throw it, and I don't think
they crack a tank. Finally we have two SA-18 shoulder-launched
SAMs with nothing but vultures for targets."

"I brought twenty pounds of C-4," Bolan said. "Make two
satchel charges out of it."

"Copy that."

"You find any bottles like I asked?"

Lkhümbengarav grinned again. "The good people here are
all Christians and pagans. I have ten empty whiskey, brandy
and gin bottles."

"Draw fuel, fill the bottles three-quarters full and top it with
motor oil and liquid soap from the relief supplies Dr. Boswerth
brought."

"I have made a Molotov cocktail before, Striker."

"You do it Mongol-style, Lucky. I don't mind."

Ceallach piped up. "You know those bloody tanks, Striker?"

"I do."

"Know what concerns me more, then?" the Briton asked.

"That technical with the quad-mounted 23s?" Bolan returned.

"They outrange everything. Minute we pop up to shoot, they
can bloody scour the canyon walls from range."

"I've been thinking about that."

"Thoughts, hell, Striker. They haunt my bloody dreams."

"Well, they're antiaircraft guns," Bolan stated.

Ceallach stared blankly. "And?"

"Well, if Mnan has the bad taste to use antiaircraft weapons
on ground targets, I say we fight fire with fire."

"Come again?" Ceallach inquired.

"The SA-18s, Scotty."

Everyone looked at the two Chinese shoulder-launched anti-aircraft missiles.

The Mongolian lost his grin. "You want to fire them at ground targets?"

"Why not?"

"A diesel truck doesn't generate enough heat. The infrared seeker can't lock."

"It has iron sights, doesn't it? So theoretically you could just fire it ballistically."

"The sights are for leading the target, but technically—"

"And it has a proximity fuse, so technically you don't actually have to hit the target."

Lkhümbengarav considered this new weird and wonderful line of thought.

"And technically," Bolan continued, "it has a range of 4,000 meters. That's, what? Three miles and some change, right, Lucky?"

"About that."

"And since it has a rocket motor, it's going to fly in a straight line so you don't have to adjust for drop."

"You're insane," the Mongolian said, but he was smiling again.

"In the eighties the Afghanis successfully used British Blowpipe surface-to-air missiles against Soviet BMP and BTR-series APCs."

Onopkov nodded and lit a cigarette. "This is true."

"You're going to trade a quad-mounted 23 with a SAM at over a mile?" Lkhümbengarav regarded Bolan with a mixture of horror and respect.

"No, I'm just going to grease that quad-mounted 23 tomorrow so Scotty can get the sleep he needs tonight. And you're coming with me."

The Mongolian's face went blank.

Bolan turned to Ceallach. "You happy?"

"Well, I'm bloody well intrigued."

Bolan looked to Shaq. "How many people do you have under arms?"

Shaq stopped short of thrusting out his chest proudly. "Twenty youths and women, ready and willing to fight, Striker."

"Lucky, issue every volunteer a rifle and put them through their paces. They can each have three magazines of practice ammo, and then put their weapons on semiauto and keep them there."

"Copy that."

"Rad, I am going to need you sniping all day long," Bolan told him.

The Serb grimaced. "I can barely hobble."

"That's why you and T-Lo are going to mount double on a bike. He's going to ferry you and carry you from position to position. When it hits the fan, it'll be a rolling shoot and scoot," Bolan stated.

You could see Mrda doing the math on his perforated posterior. "I am going to need drugs."

"I've got stuff that will blow your mind."

"Pain free, and shooting sharp, from dawn until dusk." Mrda nodded as he accepted the mission. "I can worry about the damage later."

Bolan looked around his little army. "We have only one shot at this. We break their assault or we don't. No backup is coming. There's a lot to do before dawn tomorrow. There's going to be a lot of team and assignment changes, so listen up."

18

"You are insane," Lkhümbengarav said again.

Bolan shouldered his SA-18 surface-to-air missile and pushed the arming switch. "Tell me this isn't fun."

"Like Scotty said, GI." Lkhümbengarav raised his range-finding binoculars. "I'm bloody well intrigued."

Bolan and the Mongolian knelt on the rim of the canyon. The sun rose in all of its glory, painting the scrub below pink. Some distance north and below, Chinese, Sudanese and Janjaweed were arrayed in battle order for the assault on the oasis. Diesel smoke rose in thin plumes as the tanks warmed up their engines. Eight tanks, three trucks, three technicals, six armored SUVs and about a hundred horsemen stood ready to invade. The scout lowered his range-finding binoculars. "Almost exactly one kilometer. Figure that missile is averaging six hundred meters per second? You got a good eight seconds of flight time. Lot of a hang time, GI."

Lkhümbengarav was right, Bolan knew. A lot could happen in eight seconds. He eyed Ceallach's technical nemesis. The Russian ZIL truck was the equivalent of an old American military two-and-one-half-ton flatbed. The quad-mounted 23 mm automatic cannon squatted on the flatbed like a huge, horrible and definitely hostile four-armed insect. Bolan laid the eye of his wrath upon the technical and activated his seeker. The Chinese-made missile gave off a hollow tone.

"Told you." The Mongolian sighed. "The technical is too cold. The seeker doesn't recognize any viable heat signatures. It wants a jet engine."

"Then we're just going to have to go ballistic."

"As far as I can tell, you went ballistic the second you hit the Sudan."

Bolan peered long and hard through the crude ring and post-backup sights hanging off the side of the missile tube. "Talk like that will get you a date to the prom, Lucky."

The Mongolian's eyebrows bunched. "What does *prom* mean?"

"It means, let's dance." Bolan pressed his firing button. There was almost no recoil. The Executioner felt a shudder as the missile sizzled out of the tube. The infrared seeker emitted another noise as it failed to pick up a target and continued on a straight course.

Bolan lowered his launcher and watched his missile draw its smoking line through the dawn. Firing a missile like this was kind of like playing pool. The faster you hit the ball the more you magnified any mistake. By the same token the longer the shot was, the bigger your mistakes grew. At five seconds Bolan could tell he was slightly off. Down below people had noticed the smoke and back blast of the launched missile and began wildly jumping up and down, pointing or running for cover. The technical blew diesel smoke as the driver noticed his dilemma and rammed the truck into gear. The heat seeker continued to whine about its inability to find anything of interest in the 3–5 micrometer infrared spectrum range.

The delayed impact, however, found the diesel truck and its four 23 mm automatic cannons to be a satisfyingly large source of ferrous metal and detonated when it came within thirty meters.

The detonation wasn't particularly spectacular, but the expanding fragmentation cloud riddled the cab, and thousands of ricochets winked pleasingly across the cannons like fireflies.

The Mongolian stopped just short of jumping up and down and clapping his hands. "I want a date to the prom!"

"Hand me the spare," Bolan said. He shouldered the launcher Lkhümbengarav gave him. The truck's engine was still running, and there was no guarantee the shrapnel had damaged the cannons sufficiently. They would push the thing into the canyon by hand if they had to to bring that kind of firepower to bear.

A brave soul ran forward and pulled the dead man out of the cab and leaped in. Bolan lined up his sights with the truck as smoke began to curl up from under the hood. The seeker peeped happily as the burning engine spiked into targeting wavelength. Bolan fired and his missile streaked unerring toward its target. At the same time, eight 100 mm tank cannon rose to point at their position on the ridgeline. The SA-18 had target lock and it slammed straight into the technical's grille with a much more exciting detonation. The hood rose on a column of fire and the cab blew out. The crumpled ruin dropped on its burning nose as both tires blasted out in different directions and the axle snapped. Bolan tossed aside the spent launcher. "Time to go!"

The Executioner dropped and took a sleigh ride on his rear end down the steep gravelly slope that lead to the ridge. Cannon shells slammed into the ridgeline behind them. Bolan got his feet underneath him and ran to the bottom of the slope as rock and dirt began to rain down. He clicked his com link as he ran. "Goose! Target neutralized! We are engaged!"

"Copy that," Pienaar replied. "All units in position."

As the thunder of the cannonade died, Bolan could hear the rumble of diesels in the distance. "Here they come!"

"HERE THEY COME," Mrda reported.

Bolan squatted behind a boulder with a Chinese stick grenade in his hand and listened to the sound of advancing armor echo in the canyons. "Copy that. Disposition?"

"They split up their forces. You have one platoon of tanks coming down directly on your position. They have three SUVs with them and a mixed force of infantry at platoon strength. Tanks are not buttoned down. All have their top hatch open and the heavy machine gun manned. SUVs are similarly deployed. Two have machine guns and two have grenade launchers."

Bolan thought he knew his enemies' minds.

The dawn attack on the technical with the SAMs had been good for a little shock and awe, but even if Bolan had more mis-

siles they would be useless against tanks. Rao would be well versed on how Bolan had brought the Falcons' AFV to heel with his sniper. That had been a one-trick pony, as well. Rao knew the only thing Bolan had for a stand-up fight was Rover 1 and its recoilless antitank gun. Bolan knew Rao would be willing to sacrifice an entire platoon of tanks to engage and destroy it.

Rao's problem was that Bolan had no plan whatsoever to give him a stand-up fight.

"What about horsemen, Rad?"

"Negative, Striker. None in sight."

Bolan frowned. "The tanks have scouts out front?"

"Three-man team. Approximately fifty meters ahead of the lead tank. Dressed like Sudanese regulars."

"You have a line of fire?"

"Copy that."

"Take them."

Mrda's rifle cracked three times in rapid succession. The heavy antiaircraft machine guns on the tank's turret tops ripped into life.

"Scouts down!" Mrda called. "Tanks surging forward! Coming straight at you!"

"Where's the infantry?"

"Hanging back! Waiting for the tanks to punch through the suspected ambush!"

Bolan had been betting his life on that. He heard the whine of the treadlinks as the armored behemoths bore down on his position.

"Thirty meters…twenty…ten…" Mrda reported. "Five—"

Bolan leaped out from behind his rock. The canyon was only wide enough for one tank at a time. The man behind the heavy machine gun in the turret gaped in shock as Bolan charged forward and vaulted onto the bow of the tank. The tanker tried to bring his ponderous AA gun to bear. The Executioner shoved the barrel aside and swung the Chinese stick grenade in his hand like a steel-balled blackjack. The gunner flopped backward in his hatch with a broken jaw. Bolan pulled the string fuse igniter in the handle and dropped the grenade down between the gunner's knees.

The machine gunner in the second tank's turret stared at Bolan in horror and brought his weapon down from covering the ridgeline. Slapping leather for his Beretta, the big American put a three-round burst through the man's chest. The gunner collapsed over his weapon. Bolan dropped behind the turret as the second tank's coaxial gun tore into life to try to hose him off the hull. Men screamed below his boots as the grenade within detonated and the steel compartment of the tank became a shrapnel containment coffin. The tank slowed to a halt as the driver was shredded.

Bolan leaped from the prow and ran for his rock for dear life.

The second tank rammed the lead tank. Metal screamed as the stricken tank was shoved forward. The second tank's coax scoured Bolan's rock to pin him down, but without a man in the turret, what the commander of the second tank didn't see through his periscope was Ching emerging from a cleft of rock on his flank. Ching pulled the rip cord on one of the two satchel charges Lkhümbengarav had cooked up and flung it beneath the second tank's prow. The second tank plowed on, shoving the lead tank forward and spraying bullets for Bolan. The satchel charge disappeared beneath its hull.

Smoke blasted out from beneath the second tank and fire funneled up out of her turret hatch like a volcano as ten pounds of C-4 tore her belly open and turned her insides into a blast furnace. The enemy now had a two-tank pileup. "Now, Lucky!" Bolan roared.

The Mongolian charged around the next bend in the canyon carrying the dismounted grenade launcher from the Rover. He ran up and slammed its bipod across Bolan's rock and began firing. The launcher sent a string of grenades arcing over the two wrecked tanks and into the SUVs and infantry in a six-round mix of frags and white phosphorus. The screams of the seared and shredded filled the canyon. Lkhümbengarav ejected his spent drum and clicked in a fresh one. "Another salvo?"

"No." Bolan took a Willie Pete grenade out of his load-bearing vest, aimed the bomb and threw it against the lead tank to block any surviving infantry from sneaking through for a little while. He clicked his com link. "Goose, any eyes on Mnan and his cavalry?"

"No sign of them, Striker."

Bolan was starting to get a bad feeling. He knew Yellow Mnan was up to something, and it would be two hours before he had satellite imaging of the oasis. He nodded at Ching and Lkhüm-bengarav. "Fall back to the next position. Let's find that other tank platoon."

"TWO OF MY TANKS!" Major Rahim Akeel was shrieking in a very undignified fashion. The fact that he was short, fat, chinless and sported a disastrous comb-over wasn't helping. "They have destroyed two of my tanks! Fifteen of my men are dead! How am I to explain this?"

Osmani grunted. "The victorious need explain nothing."

Rao nodded at Osmani's unexpected wisdom. The Falcon command sergeant watched the two hulks burn. Their store of cannon shells had all exploded in a string of secondary explosions, distorting the lines of their hulls in rippling blackened bulges and ragged blown-out holes. Machine-gun ammunition continued to cook off intermittently. Some of it spalled out the open hatches and torn holes. "Do not bother trying to push through, Major Akeel. Back up your surviving tanks." Rao had lost one of his SUVs and all hands within to a direct hit from a white-phosphorus grenade with the top hatch open.

"Where in the Nine Hells is Mnan!" Akeel roared.

Rao regarded the little major frostily. "What if I told you I gave him the opportunity to leave and he did?"

"What!"

Rao ignored Akeel and sent forth his orders across the communication web. "Send second platoon full forward," Rao ordered. "Drive on the oasis and engage the enemy. Let nothing stop you."

AGENT LACOSTE WASN'T HAPPY. "They come! Tanks! Two abreast down the northwest arm!" Bolan had been expecting that. The ability to send two tanks forward side by side was just too good an advantage to give up. "Composition?"

"Four tanks! Two abreast in the lead, the two behind singly making a T formation. Three SUVs behind! Single file! Infantry trotting alongside! I count thirty!"

"Copy that, LaCoste! Range to kill zone?"

"Two hundred meters and closing!"

"You hear that, Goose?"

"Clear as crystal, Striker! Awaiting fire mission!"

It had nearly broken Lkhümbengarav's heart but the previous day Bolan had wasted one of three remaining confiscated mortar shells and told him to drop it in the northwest arm of the canyon complex where tanks could move two at a time. The Mongolian had dropped his bomb with aplomb while Bolan had timed its flight. Afterward Shaq, Mesach and Abendengo had scrupulously filled in the bomb crater and erased all signs of the hit. Bolan clambered up the low crag to LaCoste's observation post. He saw the enemy armor column moving forward with purpose. "LaCoste, give me their speed."

The agent scanned through the range-finding binoculars Bolan had issued her. "Approximately ten kilometers per hour."

Bolan nodded to himself and set the stopwatch function on his phone and pulled up a window to type in a timing ratio based on the previous day's mortar-firing flight time. The average human jogging speed was about six miles per hour, and the armor didn't want to outstrip the infantry.

"Fifty meters!" LaCoste reported.

Bolan stared at his stopwatch and his algorithm. "Start ranging by fives, LaCoste."

"Copy that! Forty-five…forty…thirty-five…thirty…twenty-five…"

"Fire!" Bolan ordered. Back in the oasis he heard the dim thumps as Pienaar sent the two remaining mortar rounds arcing into the air. Bolan watched his stopwatch tick off seconds and his firing algorithm crunch numbers. Given the two rounds being fired about a second apart and the tanks' rate of speed, he'd counted on a five- to ten-meter round dispersal.

LaCoste looked up into the sky. "What has—"

The first mortar bomb hit the ground in front of the two tanks and nearly directly between them. Both tank drivers predictably slammed on their brakes, but thirty-six-ton tanks didn't stop on a dime. A second later the back deck of the right-hand tank disappeared in a blast of black smoke. Spare ammunition was stored in the back of a Type 69 tank. A second later the turret of the tank popped like a champagne cork and rose skyward on a pillar of orange pulsing smoke. LaCoste howled like a banshee in victory.

"Good work, LaCoste. Goose, direct hit. Tank destroyed."

"Magic!" the South African shouted. "Mortar is dry, Striker."

"Copy that."

Ochoa called across the link. "You want Rover 1 to come forward?"

Bolan watched as the smoke cleared. The turret man in the left-hand tank lay collapsed over his cover hatch. The blast and burning metal spewing from his platoon partner had left his flesh a smoking ruin. The tank driver beneath him ground gears and started forward. One of the two tanks behind skirted the smoldering hulk and pulled up alongside to reestablish the Chinese wall of steel.

"Negative, Sancho. Enemy still has five tanks. We're going to do a little more damage if we can before we fall back. Be ready, when it happens it's going to happen fast."

"Copy that. Holding position."

"Lucky, T.C.? I hate to do this to you."

"Ready, Striker," they both confirmed.

Bolan unlimbered his rifle and took aim at the machine gunner in the turret of the new right-hand tank. He waited as they approached the bend in the canyon. Once the Executioner fired he would announce his and LaCoste's aerie to the world.

"LaCoste, get out of here. Link up with Russo and Val at Rover 2's position."

"But I can range you and—"

"Go!"

LaCoste scooped up her rifle and scrambled down the back slope. The third tank in the platoon skirted the tank Pienaar's mortar had totaled and fell back into T formation. The SUVs filled in from behind. Bolan's rifle cracked and the machine gunner in the turret hatch flopped. "T.C.! Lucky! Now! Now! Now!"

Lkhümbengarav came out of cover with an RPG shouldered. He took a heart-stopping extra second to aim as the turrets of both tanks turned on him and fired. His rocket-propelled grenade hurtled down the canyon and slammed into the left-hand tank dead-on. The shaped-charge warhead exploded spectacularly against the vehicle's frontal glacis armor. The tank rumbled out of the smoke with a spectacular but apparently nonlethal blackened dent in its prow. Ching took the opportunity to step out from behind a rock and sling a satchel charge beneath the treads of the right-hand tank.

The vehicle rolled forward in blissful ignorance and then shuddered as fire and smoke blasted out from beneath her hull. She took an out-of-control right turn and slammed into the canyon wall. The Mongolian shoved a fresh rocket into his tube.

"Lucky, get out of there!" Bolan ordered.

The surviving tank's turret turned on the Mongolian, who stood his ground and aimed.

"Move!" Bolan roared.

Lkhümbengarav's RPG round ripped from his tube. In the two seconds of flight time, the tank's coaxial machine gun shredded the Mongolian mercenary like confetti. The rocket-propelled grenade slammed into the tank's compromised glacis plate, and this time the shaped-charge warhead pierced the rolled-steel armor. The tank came to a smoldering stop as the incinerated occupants ceased all functions. A cold wind blew through Bolan clicked his com link. "Two tanks down. Lucky is gone. All units fall back to your next position."

19

Bolan drew up his battle plan. Ching, Tshabalala and LaCoste made up his forward line. Ochoa was in command of Rover 1 and Onopkov had Rover 2. The Kong brothers were driving and loading for Ochoa. Nelsonne was driving for the Russian. Pienaar and Mrda were back at the oasis with Boswerth and the refugees. Bolan coordinated the battle with his phone and his com. "Listen up, they have three tanks, three technicals and five of those Chinese SUVs."

Ceallach wandered over and thrust the two Chinese antitank grenades through his belt like a pirate. He popped the bicep on his good arm. "And I can throw a grenade farther than anyone else in this bloody outfit!" He began loading his pockets and his sling with grenades of every description.

"Striker!" Kurtzman called. "I have movement! Looks like they're putting their technicals in front."

"Show me." Bolan eyed his phone. There was definitely movement on the satellite image. The enemy had gathered at the northwest arm of the canyon. "They're reversing strategy. They're going to send the light vehicles forward as skirmishers. When we're fully engaged, the tanks will come in firing over them." Bolan frowned. "Bear, show me the west arm of the canyon."

The satellite swept westward and down. Bolan made out the two smoldering tank wrecks. "Hold image!" He watched a pair of men scamper across the scant open ground and disappear under the canyon shelf. They were swiftly followed by another pair and then another. "Show me the west canyon entrance." Bolan observed three empty Sudanese military trucks.

"All right, everyone listen up. We have infantry massing in the west canyon arm. I'm thinking it's this Major Akeel's men backed up by as many as Osmani can spare. In fact I'm betting Osmani is leading them. Once we're engaged with the armor, they'll attack our flank. Shaq, its time for you and your volunteers to step up. Rad, you're going to back them up. Take the .30. That canyon is only wide enough for one tank. My advice is once they attack, fill the whole place with white phosphorus and frags and shoot anything that comes staggering out."

The Serb nodded.

"T.C.? You're my RPG man."

"I saw what happened to your last one."

Bolan ignored the remark. "T-Lo, I'm taking one of the anti-tank rifle grenades. You're taking the other. LaCoste, I'm issuing you two of the rifle grenades. They're frags. They may or may not stop the Chinese trucks, and they'll be useless against the tanks. If you use them on a vehicle, try to do it at close range, or if the SUVs deploy men. Scotty?" Bolan shook his head at the Briton, who was festooned with grenades like they were Christmas-tree ornaments. "You're bowling googlies at the tanks, SUVs or whatever the hell else strikes your fancy."

A few laughs broke out among the team.

Ceallach snorted. "I've got a question. Where the bloody hell is Mnan and his bloody hundred Huns, then?"

Bolan spoke into his phone. "Bear, any sign of Mnan?"

"Negative, Striker, and a hundred horses aren't very easy to conceal. Even in the canyons."

"Go to a wider field. Look outside the canyons."

"Which direction?

"First scan west."

"Striker!" Kurtzman suddenly sounded excited. "Eyes on Mnan and his horsemen. They're heading due west at the gallop."

"All of them?"

"Looks like the entire horde has pulled up stakes."

"Show me." The satellite image on Bolan's screen shifted.

He saw the outline of a horde of horsemen about the size of ants moving at speed and heading west.

"Cowardly booger," Ceallach commented.

"Bear, keep an eye on them when you can. This may be a feint."

"Copy that, Striker."

Bolan slung his sniper rifle and took up a rifle. He topped it with his last frag grenade and stuck the antitank round into a pouch on his load-bearing vest. "Let's do this."

THE TECHNICAN WENT UP on two wheels and nearly crashed as it threaded the needle between the two ruined tanks. Bolan noted with interest that men in Sudanese army uniforms occupied it. Mnan might just have bugged out after all. The gunner in the back had a twin-mounted pair of .30-caliber machine guns and he sprayed them wildly in all directions. "LaCoste! Take him!"

Agent LaCoste popped up out of her spider hole. Her grenade blew off her rifle, and the recoil nearly knocked her over. The bomb sailed through the windshield of the Toyota's sawed-off cab and detonated. Driver, gunner and loader were shredded. The pickup went up on two wheels again and this time it rolled.

SUVs began threading the needle. Men in Falcon uniforms stood in the sunroofs behind general-purpose machine guns searching for targets. Bolan took aim with his rifle. Behind the SUVs he heard the slap-slap-slap of an automatic grenade launcher.

"Grenades!" Bolan shouted. His team hunkered down in their fighting holes or behind rocks as grenades rained down at random. "Val! Rover 2!"

Rover 2 tore around the bend in the canyon behind them with Nelsonne behind the wheel and Onopkov behind the big .50. The heavy machine gun cycled into life and tore through the lead SUV's grille. The Russian raised his aim and hammered off another burst through the windshield. Bolan rose from behind his boulder and put a bullet through the machine gunner. The vehicle slowed to a halt, and two Sudanese soldiers leaped out of the back doors. Two more SUVs swerved around either side of their stricken fellow. Onopkov opened up again.

"Taking the shot!" Tshabalala called.

"Go!" Bolan replied. The South African rose and fired his frag. The rifle grenade spiraled through the air and hit the closest SUV broadside. The vehicle slewed in the sand but kept coming.

"Taking the shot!" LaCoste called.

"Go!"

LaCoste fired straight-on. Bolan drilled two bullets through the armored windshield as the French agent rose and fired her second grenade. The frag hit the compromised armor glass, and the rest of the windows lit up as most of the blast and shrapnel funneled into the interior. Ceallach squatted in the shadow of one of the stricken tanks forming the bottleneck. It was good cover except for the fact that it absolutely depended on no one looking backward at any time. Bolan saw him peer through a gap between the tank hulk and the canyon wall. Ceallach clicked his com link. "Here come the tanks, Striker."

"Status?"

"Buttoned up, lighter vehicles leading."

"Copy that! Sancho! Be ready!"

"Locked and loaded, Striker!" Ochoa replied.

Bolan did the math. Three tanks, three SUVs and a technical remained. He raised his head at the sound of massed gunfire in the distance. Mrda reported in. "Striker! We have Sudanese infantry engaging!"

"Copy that! Keep me advised!" Bolan grimaced as a second salvo of grenades came across the tank hulks. The Chinese frags hit the sand with soft thuds and detonated like whips cracking. Nelsonne screamed.

Bolan looked over his boulder and saw smoke rising from LaCoste's spider hole. "Russo! Report! Russo!"

The SUVs threaded the hulks in a serpentine wave. Onopkov opened up with the heavy gun and chewed the front end of the lead one to bits. The machine gun fell silent as the Russian racked it open and slapped a new belt of ammo into the smoking action. The second SUV plowed through. Ceallach bowled a concussion grenade beneath its wheels in passing. The grenade detonated beneath its chassis, snapping its axle. The bumper dropped and shoveled up dirt. The Briton pulled his machine pistol and shot the roof gunner.

As the tanks blasted through the barricade of their dead brethren, Ceallach avoided being crushed by inches. He heaved himself on top of the shattered tank and hugged the turret. The lead tank simply saw a fallen SUV and rolled right over it. The screams of the men inside were lost as the thirty-six-ton tank flattened the Chinese truck like a beer can.

"Now, Sancho! Bring her up!" Bolan ordered. "T.C.! Take the shot!"

Ching had a slope of slick rock fifty yards from the bottleneck. He rose, laid his launch tube and fired. The RPG rocket hit the turret of the lead tank dead-on. The tank rolled on through the smoke with a blackened dent in its turret. Ching dropped flat as the 100 mm cannon fired and tore away a tombstone-size slab of slick rock from over his head. "T.C.!"

"I am okay!" Ching hunched, then loaded his last rocket as a second cannon shell tore another giant divot from his cover. Onopkov poured fire into the last SUV, which shuddered to a stop as he shot it to pieces.

"Rover 2! Fall back!" Bolan ordered.

Nelsonne ground gears and put the Rover into Reverse.

A third salvo of grenades soared into Bolan's team's territory. Nelsonne yelled something in French. Bolan looked back to see the front of Rover 2 blackened and the Frenchwoman clutching her face. Rover 1 slid around the bend into view. The tube of the recoilless antitank gun pivoted smoothly under Ochoa's steady hand and the weapon belched fire from both ends. His round hit the lead tank dead-on in the turret. The turret hatch blasted upward, and the cannon barrel sagged down as the vehicle ground to a halt. Shartai slammed open the breech and plucked out the smoking shell. Haitham shoved the Rover into gear to present a moving target.

"Val! Get Russo out of there!"

Onopkov shouted at Nelsonne but stayed behind his weapon.

He poured rounds into the next tank to keep it occupied. The Frenchwoman managed to grab her rifle and flop from behind the wheel. Bolan leveled his rifle with the antitank grenade attached. The rifle butt slammed into his shoulder and a second later the bomb detonated below the cannon barrel. The tank ignored Bolan's grenade and fired its cannon.

Onopkov disappeared as Rover 2 went sky-high.

The two remaining tanks ground forward. A coaxial gun stitched the sand, seeking Nelsonne. The French agent just managed to flop behind a rock that resembled a filing cabinet laid on its side.

Ching rose with his RPG and fired.

His rocket streaked into the tank he and Bolan had both hit before. The detonation smeared around the hemisphere of the turret in a blanket of smoke and fire.

The tank rumbled on, unstoppable.

Rover 1 slammed to a halt and Ochoa aimed his reloaded recoilless antitank gun. The weapon roared, and his round struck the tank just below the turret on the diagonal. Orange fire flashed as the round penetrated, and a second later the tank went up as all steel tanks would when they took a round through the magazine.

The last tank rumbled forward, and a technical emerged from the tank hulks behind it. The technical sported a Russian 30 mm automatic grenade launcher. The launcher began thumping in a grenade sweep across Bolan's line. The tank rolled forward, immune to any friendly grenade fragments, and its turret turned on Rover 1. Ochoa and Haitham desperately slammed a fresh round into the recoilless gun. The driver ground gears to put Rover 1 in Reverse.

The weren't going to make it.

Tshabalala rose and fired the last antitank rifle grenade. The munition spun straight and true into the tank's starboard side. The tank ignored the blow and fired its main gun at Rover 1, which was a yard away from cover as the cannon shell blew through her front grille.

"Sancho!" Tshabalala screamed. "Sancho!" He fired his magazine dry and dropped into his spider hole as the tank turned its attention on him. The tank fired its cannon, and rock and dirt geysered skyward.

"T-Lo!" Bolan knew it was useless but prayed for a miracle. "T-Lo!"

His team was being cut to pieces.

Ching rose and hurled a hand grenade at the tank. The concussion grenade did little more than blacken the dull green paint. "Striker!" Ching pulled the pin on a second grenade. "Get out of there!"

Bolan pulled the pins on a pair of his own grenades and charged instead.

The technical began to fire another salvo of grenades, which suddenly ended as Ceallach walked up behind it and tossed a frag in the back bed. The bomb detonated and killed the gunner and loader. The Briton tossed a second lethal orb through the open window of the cab and ducked behind the rear bumper as it blew out the windows and the life of the man driving.

"T.C.!" Bolan yelled. "Diversion for Scotty!"

Ching hurled another grenade and dropped down as the tank's main gun fired. His ramp of slick rock was swiftly becoming rubble. Bolan sprinted into range. His progress was noted and the tank's turret spun to put its gun on him. The big American threw his grenade. The white phosphorus bomb hit the tank square on the slanted frontal arc of its armor. The vehicle was buttoned up, and the burning metal had no chance of inflicting damage on any part of the tank except its paint job. However, the prow of the tank disappeared in the ensuing white smoke and skyrocketing burning metal streamers.

Bolan jinked hard left and threw himself down as the tank fired blindly at him. The sonic crack of a tank shell passing two feet overhead tried to make Bolan's eardrums meet in the middle of his head. Coax fire followed, but it was scything in the wrong direction. Bolan rose and ran forward. Ceallach walked up behind the tank, then tossed one of his antitank grenades on top of the vehicle's bow deck. Like all tanks, its top armor was thinnest. The grenade detonated with a thunderclap.

The tank commander noted the blast and turned his turret

on the new threat. The Briton ran in recklessly close, he took an extra second to judge his toss and laid his second grenade next to the first. The blast slapped him back like an invisible hand and sat him in the sand. The tank bucked and came to a stop. Russian tanks kept their engines in the back, and it looked as though Ceallach had dealt the V-12 diesel a blow.

The turret kept turning.

Bolan charged the tank. Heat rolled off the prow in a wave from the front deck coated in burning phosphorus. He ignored the heat and burning smoke and jumped. Hooking an arm over the 100 mm barrel, he let it carry him toward the bow, ignoring the searing heat coming off the barrel. The turret continued to turn and deposited him onto the tank's blackened back deck. A scorched dent the size of a trash can lid cratered the steel, and a smoking hole the size of a fist marked where Ceallach's second grenade had penetrated. Bolan could hear men shouting below and a squirt of chemical fire extinguisher puffed up out of the hole. The Executioner opened his hand and his grenade's cotter lever pinged away.

He dropped his concussion grenade down the hole.

The lethal radius of the grenade blast was five yards. The steel hull of the tank left the concussion wave with nowhere to go. The tank shuddered as its interior became an echo chamber of death.

Bolan slid off the tank.

Ceallach made an effort to stand and failed. The big American dropped to a knee. "You all right?"

Ceallach blinked. "What?"

"Are you all right?"

He blinked again. "What?"

Bolan peered into the Briton's eyes. Both pupils were still the same size, and he wasn't leaking blood from any opening in his head. He took Ceallach's machine pistol out of its holster and pressed it into his hand. "Hold on to this."

"What?"

Bolan spoke slowly and exaggerated his mouth motions. "Hold…on…to…this!"

Ceallach looked at the weapon for the first time. "Right!"

Bolan unslung his sniper rifle. He could feel his left inner arm blistering. He walked over to Ching, who was taking deep breaths. "I had read about Panzer Fever, now I know what it means."

Panzer Fever was a World War II term. It described the infectious terror of men facing oncoming tanks with nothing that could stop them.

Bolan nodded. "You did good."

"I have read about men charging tanks." Ching stared long and hard. "In books."

The Executioner looked back. "Russo!"

"I'm a mess!"

Bolan walked over to LaCoste's position. The agent's spider hole had become her grave. Ching stood over Tshabalala's position, shaking his head. The 100 mm shell had doubled the size of the South African's fighting position. A mangled rifle and a boot were about all that were recognizable.

Nelsonne joined him. The only thing keeping the beautiful French agent's left eyebrow attached to her face were her fingers. The eye was swollen and the flesh of her cheek below a raccoon patch of bruising. "How many did we lose?"

"You, T.C., Scotty and me are alive."

Ceallach joined his teammates. Bolan eyed the Englishman once more and spoke slowly. "You okay?"

The Briton shouted at the top his lungs like the newly deaf on the battlefield often did. "Well, I'm bloody deaf, then, aren't I?" He flapped his blood-dotted sling. "Bleeding again!"

Bolan clicked his com link. "Rad, report." Static greeted him. "Rad, report."

The com link clicked and crackled. Shaq answered. "Striker?"

"Shaq, report."

"Mr. Rad is dead." Shaq's voice broke. "My brother Mesach is dead. He died fighting. We put the enemy in a cross fire like you said. We killed many of them. We threw grenades and firebombs like you said. We stopped them. But they fired grenades back in retreat. Mr. Rad told us to take cover, but he was injured. He was slow. I should have—"

"You won, Shaq. Your brother died to save your people. So did Rad. Remember that."

Shaq sobbed. "I will, Striker."

"Hold position."

Iron came back into Shaq's voice. "I will, Striker."

"Goose, looks like we stopped them. Enemy armor destroyed. Falcons destroyed. Sudanese regulars in retreat." Bolan waited but Pienaar didn't respond. "Goose, report."

Ching spoke low. "I have a bad feeling."

"Bear!" Bolan called. "Show me Mnan's cavalry."

Kurtzman came back instantly. "Do you—"

"Do it!"

Bolan watched his screen. Once more he saw the shifting shape of the horsemen heading west. "Give me higher resolution, Bear."

"How close do you want to get?"

"Put me in the saddle."

"One second." The view narrowed as the satellite peered ever more closely at the Janjaweed cavalry. Bolan's blood went cold as the satellite swept the retreating cavalry from about a hundred feet overhead. By Bolan's count about every third saddle was empty.

Bolan's com link crackled. Rao's voice spoke. "I thought soldiers like you only existed in movies. It has been a singular honor to have been your opponent."

The Executioner said nothing.

"But you have lost," Rao continued. "Surrender now. If you do not, I will shoot the South African. Then I will shoot every doctor except Bosworth. Then I will begin shooting the refugees in groups of five every five minutes."

Bolan said nothing.

"Let me add that Dr. Bosworth can be useful to us without legs and many other body parts," Rao added. "Do you doubt me?"

Bolan took a long breath and steeled himself for what was to come. "No."

"You have twenty minutes before I start killing."

20

It was a hostage situation of biblical proportions.

Bolan knelt on the crag with his sniper rifle. His lungs burned from his canyon run. His seared left arm was an agony. The soldier had debated whether painkillers or the pain would be more distractive to good shooting. He had chosen his old friend pain. Sometimes it could be remarkably clarifying. The refugees had been placed kneeling in the execution position 5x5 just as Rao had threatened. Bolan scanned from his position and counted thirty Janjaweed along with Mnan, Rao and one of his Falcons.

Bolan had about thirty refugees back in the canyons with Ching to lead them, but they had seen their first battle only an hour ago. Nelsonne and Ceallach were with them, but the Briton and the French agent were in bad shape. They would attack if he called for it, but the battle would entail horrific casualties, and nothing would stop Mnan and his men from hosing down the hostages left, right and sideways.

The Executioner checked his watch. He had picked out a sniper spot overlooking the oasis. He had arrived with about a minute to spare out of the twenty Rao had given him.

Rao raised Pienaar's commandeered com link. The Falcon beside the South African held a pistol pointed at the back of Pienaar's head. Bosworth knelt beside him. They had forced her to her knees despite the fact that she had a hole in her leg. Rao scanned the canyon rims and held the com link slightly away as he raised his voice to bounce it off the canyon walls. "I believe you can hear me, American! I believe you can see me!"

Bolan spoke through the com link. "I hear you."

"I will make you a deal. I care nothing for the refugees or the other doctors, or even your surviving teammates. I am taking Dr. Bosworth, you and the Chinese traitor Tien Ching with me. I will let everyone else live. I give you my word. I will pay Mr. Mnan good money to let them flee south unmolested."

"He's lying." Ching's voice came low and steely across the backup channel. "We attack now, Striker. Say the word. Shaq and his people are down with this. We have bayonets fixed."

Bolan acknowledged on the same channel. "T.C.?"

"Yes, Striker."

"Hold that thought."

"Copy that, Striker. Holding thought. Holding position."

Rao shouted out. "American! Your time is up!"

Bolan took a long breath and let it out.

Rao spoke quietly, but clicked his com so Bolan could hear. "Mnan, tell your men to kill the first five—" The Chinese operative staggered backward like a man who had taken a surprise claw hammer to the chest and fell down dead.

Bolan flicked his bolt and shot the Falcon standing behind Pienaar. The Falcon did both Bolan and Pienaar a favor as he dropped his pistol, clutched his chest and fell to the ground next to his sergeant commander. Bolan swung his rifle onto Mnan, but Bosworth gasped in Bolan's optic as Yellow Mnan's arm cinched beneath her chin and compressed her throat. He pressed a pistol to her head. The Executioner had known he would have to kill Rao. The sergeant commander had been a man on a mission. On the other hand Bolan had met a lot of scumbags in his life. In certain circumstances they could be made to see reason.

His voice boomed over the canyon land. "Do you know what my mission is, Mnan?"

The assembled Janjaweed looked at Mnan and around at one another nervously.

Mnan waved his pistol gleefully around the warriors surrounding him as he hugged the doctor half to death. "Your mission is to rescue this white bitch! Try it! You come down here and try it! I have thirty men! You have no chance! Attack with whatever you have! Shoot one more man! Shoot one more man and watch what happens! Surrender!"

Mnan was right. There was no way Bolan could fight his way down to the hostages. Open battle would get most of them killed. If he surrendered, it would end in torture and horror for all. Running wasn't an option.

"Go ahead!" Mnan's voice was sick with victory. "You shoot me and—"

Bolan shot Mnan. The .338 Lapua Magnum round tore away Yellow Mnan's sunglasses, his cowboy hat and the top of his head. Dr. Bosworth flinched and hugged herself as the dead albino slithered off her shoulders like a husk. Yellow Mnan's men stared for a shocked moment at the terrible six inches off the top Bolan had taken.

"My mission?" Bolan thundered. "Dr. Bosworth does not fall into enemy hands! Guess where she is right now! Go ahead! Go ahead and kill her! I'll kill her before I let you have her! Go ahead and kill my man Goose! I'll kill him before I let you feed them to the hyenas!"

The South African grinned savagely.

"Go ahead and kill your own people!" Bolan roared. "You watch what happens! You have no vehicles! No horses! Go ahead! Try to take my truck! Step behind the wheel and watch what happens.

"Surrender now!" Bolan's voice rose to godlike anger. "Or I kill anything that moves!"

The Janjaweed thugs hunched and flinched despite themselves and looked back and forth for a way out.

"Go ahead! Scatter like rabbits! You are walking out of these canyons!" Bolan bellowed. "And I am your thousand-yard shadow! Every step of the way! No one gets out alive except me!"

A Janjaweed terrorist shook his rifle in defiance. "He is bluffing! He will not—"

Bolan's .338 Magnum round punched through the man's pineal gland and took out the entire frontal lobe on the way. The rabble-rouser dropped skull-capped to the sand. "And you had better pray to the God of your forefathers if you haven't surrendered by nightfall! Because then I'm hunting with a knife! And by Allah I am taking testicles!"

A Janjaweed thug threw down his rifle. The man next to him slapped him. Bolan shot Slappy through the chest. "Live or die!" The Executioner's voice echoed across the canyon lands like God on High. "Choose!"

The Janjaweed gunners wept and cursed and shouted epithets and defiance. Then the next one threw down his weapon and chose life. Rifles clattered to the ground in a cascade of despair. Pienaar rose and picked up Mnan's pistol. He gave Boswerth a shoulder to lean on, shoved a rifle into her hands and then took back his com device from Rao. "Striker?"

"Goose, you all right?" Bolan asked.

Pienaar had other concerns. "How's my brother-in-law?"

"T-Lo died going forward, Goose. He died fighting tanks."

Pienaar cleared his throat. "Boswerth and I are bleeding rivers. We can't hold down the oasis. God knows how long the Janjaweed will stay cowed. We need backup now."

"Copy that," Bolan acknowledged. "T.C., bring your team forward. Leave Abendengo and a man to watch the back door. Keep a leash on Shaq and his people. No reprisals, and no killing unless you meet resistance. Secure the oasis. Free the doctors and get them to work on the wounded. I'm holding position until you give me the all clear."

"Copy that, Striker. Shaq Force moving forward. They understand their orders."

"Copy that, T.C." Bolan watched as Ching and his Sudanese refugee army came trotting out of the canyons and into the oasis with bayonets fixed. The Janjaweed fighters flinched and hunched, but none was foolhardy enough to go for his weapon. Ceallach and Nelsonne came walking in at a more sedate pace. The Englishman still had his machine pistol and a sling full of grenades. The Frenchwoman had wrapped her face with her torn shirtsleeve. It had already bled through. With her bayonet fixed and half her face wrapped in bloody rags, she definitely looked hostile.

Bolan spoke into his phone wearily. "Bear, tell me the canyons are clear."

"I have the Janjaweed horse horde still heading due west with no sign of stopping. I have one truck from the west canyon arm heading hard north. The other two are still there. I think Rad and Team Shaq killed everyone else with a truck driver's license. Nothing is smoking. I don't think they took the time to disable them. They just ran."

Hard north told Bolan that it was Akeel's forces fleeing for Fort Abdel, where he could once again explain another glorious retreat with honor to the high command in Khartoum. It also told him Osmani was dead or incapacitated. Osmani would have thought to destroy the remaining trucks and would have headed west. "Copy that, Bear."

Ching and Shaq Force took the oasis. There were a few gratuitous rifle butts applied to the cringing Janjaweed men, but Ching kept discipline. He put Pienaar back in command and swept the oasis from stem to stern with a picked band of Shaq's people. Bolan allowed himself to relax as Ching clicked his com link and waved at Bolan's sniper aerie.

"Oasis secure, Striker."

"Copy that, T.C."

"Striker?"

"T.C.?"

"Why don't you come down, get your arm looked at. Take a nap. I'll spell you on lookout."

Stretching his hammock between two palm trees and going lights-out for twelve hours sounded like luxury beyond the dreams of avarice. It was a luxury he couldn't afford at the moment. He would take up the first and second parts of T.C.'s offer. "Copy that."

BOLAN WALKED INTO THE infirmary tent. Five doctors were in camp and one of them had a wounded leg. There had been a gun battle and health care was being triaged. Despite his nearly godlike status among the oasis residents, Bolan and his burned arm had gone to the back of the line. The good news was that he had gotten some chow and his nap. Pienaar and Ceallach had insisted on it, and Bolan had been too tired to resist.

The soldier took a seat on a cot and stripped off his shirt. Bosworth and her people seemed to know what they were doing. They had come to fight famine and disease. Treating refugees in the Sudan had taught them all about burns, blast damage and bullet wounds. Bosworth hobbled over. Like Bolan she had responsibilities, and superficial leg wounds weren't allowed to interfere with them. She gave Bolan a smile. "Stick out your arm."

He stuck out his arm. His left inner arm and side looked like an NFL fullback whose quarterback had handed him a red-hot football and he'd run for a touchdown. Bosworth began to clean the wound. "I've heard a few secondhand stories about your fight in the canyon."

"Oh?"

"May I offer you a piece of advice?"

"Sure."

"Burning tanks are not monkey bars, Striker. You shouldn't climb on them."

Bolan sighed. "You know, you're not the first person to tell me that."

"You know, I'm not surprised." Bosworth wrapped his arm. "Mostly second-degree burns. You should heal in a couple of weeks. Infection while you're in-country is your only real concern."

"Can I give you a piece of advice?"

"Sure…"

"I have a chopper coming. Get out of the Sudan."

Bosworth's face went flat. "I have responsibilities here."

"Dr. Bosworth, the Chinese know who you are and where you are. The Sudanese have no idea what's going on down here except that something is going on. They'll be coming. You are a danger to these people."

"So what happens? After all we've done. After all the killing, we just abandon them?"

"No, I'm going to load them into the Mog and the two trucks

Major Akeel kindly left us and personally convoy them to the South Sudanese border."

Bosworth blinked. "You are, aren't you?"

"Some good people died to save them. This mission isn't over yet." Bolan's voice hardened. "Now tell me you are getting on that damn helicopter."

Bosworth's eyes were shiny. "I'm getting on the damn helicopter."

"Good, if we're done here, go pack. There's no place to land the chopper, so you and the worst of the wounded are being hoisted. Pack light."

Bosworth got her crutches under her and the waterworks turned on despite her best effort. "Striker?"

He nodded. "You're welcome."

Bosworth leaned in and kissed his cheek before leaving the tent.

Nelsonne grinned at Bolan out of her mangled face. "Well, look at you."

He lifted his chin at the woman's mangled face and grinned back. "Look at you."

She made a noise of disgust. "I do not wish to."

"Scars are sexy, and glory is forever."

Nelsonne giggled.

Bolan grew serious. "I want you on that chopper."

"You need me."

"I do, but you have a concussion. You don't want to be bouncing across the Sudan in a 4x4." Bolan shrugged. "Besides, it might look good to the boys back in Paris when you personally deliver Dr. Bosworth safely to the American Embassy."

Nelsonne grew quiet. "That is very kind of you."

"It's nothing. Besides, we have a date, and I hear French-women take a long time to get ready."

Nelsonne made a noise and circled her face with her finger. "You still want me? With my face like this?"

"Well…" Bolan scratched his chin in thought. "You'd be a two-bagger, but sure. What the hell."

Nelsonne gave him a very suspicious look. "And just what is a...*two-bagger?*"

"Well, a one-bagger is a girl who's so ugly that you have to put a bag over her head to make love to her."

"And a two-bagger..."

"A two-bagger is a girl who's so ugly that not only do you put a bag over her head to make love to her, but you put a bag over your own head in shame."

"You...are...a...pig."

Bolan nodded and rose. He had an evacuation to manage and a refugee hell-run for the South Sudanese border to lead. "See you in Bruges."

* * * * *